Jisilyn M.
Holdridge

BLUE

JESILYN HOLDRIDGE

a novel

BLUE

TATE PUBLISHING
AND ENTERPRISES, LLC

Published by Tate Publishing & Enterprises, LLC
127 E. Trade Center Terrace | Mustang, Oklahoma 73064 USA
1.888.361.9473 | www.tatepublishing.com

Tate Publishing is committed to excellence in the publishing industry. The company reflects the philosophy established by the founders, based on Psalm 68:11,
"The Lord gave the word and great was the company of those who published it."

Book design copyright © 2012 by Tate Publishing, LLC. All rights reserved.
Cover design by Rtor Maghuyop
Interior design by Nathan Harmony

Published in the United States of America

ISBN: 978-1-62147-809-6
1. Fiction / Coming Of Age
2. Fiction / Christian / General
12.09.27

ACKNOWLEDGMENTS

I would like to thank my eighth grade English teacher, who helped show me the wonders in writing.

CHAPTER 1

She was tall, smart, funny, and kind. Then again, maybe he stole that from her. She had dirty blond hair with pure blonde highlights. She had the look of the prettiest girl in the school because of the shape of her body. Her name was Meganlynn VanDeritie. She was the nicest girl in her grade and never really hated anybody, well, that was until Blue came around. He had tortured her, beaten her, and broken her, and not just on the outside but on the inside as well.

August 21, 2001, was when all of this started. The football field at Heart Middle School was big, and the band was warming up for their pre-band camp for the summer. Many people went through this every summer. Nobody ever thought that he would ever be in band. They never thought that Mr. Nolls, the band director, would ever let him in. He was a terrible trombone player. But he wanted to stay by Meganlynn.

Meganlynn VanDeritie had been in band for the three years. She was everybody's best friend, but he still got away with stealing that from her when he decided to harass her.

On the first day of pre-band camp, Meganlynn was walking into the doors of the middle school that she had just graduated from. She had a boyfriend that loved her, or at least seemed to love her, and tried his best to protect her at all times. She also had friends that would have her back and support her along whatever road she decided to take. Whether it was the long road or the short road, they would always fight for her. She, herself, was a very strong person, not only somewhat physically, but also in her mind and her emotions. It would take a lot to break her, and he knew this for a fact.

She walked in the doors and all of her friends came charging to her, hugging her and screaming in her ears. The only one that was not there was her boyfriend Justin Morgan.

Justin Morgan was a very protective boyfriend. He rarely let her in the same room as the boy who used to harass her, Blue Robenson. Justin barely knew what Blue really did to her in detail; he only knew that Blue used to sexually harass Meganlynn. He really did seem to love her for all of her flaws and all of her strengths. Justin had blonde hair with deep, blue eyes. He never looked at anyone as if he were better than him—other than Blue, that is, because he felt that he deserved that kind of attitude toward him for what he did to his girlfriend.

Blue Robenson was exactly the opposite of Justin, period. He was disrespectful and hateful. He was also tall but not good-looking, and he was one of those people that could make you feel smaller than a period on a page just by looking at him. He seemed to love Meganlynn with a passion, but he didn't love her to the point of the "for better and for worse" wedding vows sort of love. It was only a physical attraction. He didn't care what happened to Meganlynn as long as he got a girlfriend to get a reputation going. If he could get Meganlynn, it was a big reputation booster, but she had been with Justin for over a year. Blue was also black haired and brown eyed. He always looked down at the ground when facing anyone superior, but never ever looked down whenever facing a simple classmate.

There has to be some way to get around her and Justin. There just has to be another way, Blue thought to himself silently as he talked to his friend at the band camp. *Everybody has a weakness, and she can't do anything this time around. Well, she can tell her father, but I doubt that she will. They can't be that close.*

"Oh! I missed you guys so much!" Meganlynn exclaimed, running up to one of her best friends, Lizzie Margin. Lizzie was golden haired and green eyed. She was also light skinned and she always had something to talk about. She absolutely loved to talk. She also played the clarinet, and she had been playing it for about the same time as Meganlynn. She was also part of the four girls that had joined the sisterhood of their school.

The sisterhood just happened to be a small little group that one of the girls had started back when they were still in elementary school. They had all been in the same classes for years and had all just become best friends almost seemingly overnight. They all stuck together for everything and had each other's back through thick and thin.

"Oh! I missed you too!" exclaimed Lizzie.

"Meganlynn! I didn't see you there!" screamed one of her other best friends, Morgan Lovely. She was one of the most tomboyish people that the sisterhood would ever have. She never ever looked down at anybody, and never looked down when anybody was speaking to her. She was brown haired and light blue eyed. For marching band she enjoyed being in color guard, but in reality, she played the flute.

"Morgan! Oh, I've missed you!" Meganlynn cried back. These were the people that she wanted to see, but yet they were not. More than anything she wished to see, speak, and once again, be held by her boyfriend. Suddenly, Meganlynn jumped from her current position to do a one hundred-eighty degree twist to the point to where she was staring the last member of the sisterhood in the face.

There, right behind her, stood Taylor VanFork. She was a black-haired girl with grey eyes. She thought that Meganlynn was being treated like crap by Justin, and could definitely see it now that he hadn't even come over to see her yet.

"Hey sis," Taylor said holding her arms out to show Meganlynn that she wanted a hug.

"Hi," Meganlynn answered.

"Has Justin even come over and talked to you to say 'hi' or anything yet?" asked Taylor.

"No, he's just been over with all the pack of boys talking to them not even noticing me one little bit. I went over to see him, but he just ignored me, so I really don't know what his deal is," Meganlynn answered.

"Wow! What a jerk. How much longer are you going to put up with this?" Morgan asked.

"I don't know. I was going to see if he even cared enough to come over and talk to me, but so far he hasn't exactly shown me that he's still 'in love' with me," she answered, looking over at him. She couldn't believe that she was actually saying these words since he had been in love with her for the past two years. There was even a slight chance that he had even been in love with her for three years. She didn't know why she was saying it nor did she know what was going to happen to them. She took a deep breath and then looked back over at Justin.

Justin was talking to his friends and being his normal self. He had seen Meganlynn looking over at him, but since she hadn't come over to talk to him quite yet, he figured that he'd wait for her to come over and see him. He hadn't quite been as in love with her as he might have told her when they were in school, but every day that he was around her, he seemed to love her more and more. The only problem was that the opposite effect was true as well—the less he saw of her, the less he cared.

Why can't I possibly remember her face? I was supposed to be so in love with her that it wasn't even funny, but I guess I should probably get up the nerve to just break it off with her, he thought to himself. He couldn't possibly do that to her though. Somewhere deep inside of him, he just had to love her even though she wasn't calling him nor talking to him. He looked at his best friends with caring eyes for her but not for them.

"Hey." He started looking at the ground because he was ashamed of asking the question. "Do you guys think that I should break-up with Meganlynn?"

"No," answered one of his best friends, Robert. "Dude, you and Meg used to be one of the hottest couples that have ever walked the eighth grade halls. Mr. Jilging walked in on you guys, and you never got into trouble with her. I'm pretty sure that you still love her."

Justin dropped his shoulders and then looked back at the ground again.

"Yeah, maybe, but I mean I can't even remember her face whenever she's not around, and I don't miss her all that much."

"Maybe it's just because you haven't seen each other for a long time."

"But we saw each other at the practices that we had on Monday nights."

"Did you guys talk?"

"No, but still—"

"Then that's probably the reason that you can't remember her face and why you don't miss her. Just go and talk to her again and maybe then you will remember her face when she's not around, and maybe you'll start to miss her so much that you'll have to call her every second of the day."

"I hardly ever call her."

"Then maybe you should start."

"Maybe, I don't know."

"Okay band, let's get into your proper sections," Mr. Nolls, the band director, told the group as he got up in front of the band. Meganlynn sat down and looked at her music down on the stand. Blue Robenson then sat down next to Meganlynn, making her jump.

"What are you doing here?" she asked, sounding both mad and scared.

"I'm just playing my instrument," he said, looking straight into her eyes. "Please, Meg, just give me another chance. I'm not the guy that I was last year," he said, putting his hand on her hip. He left it there just long enough for Robert to see him.

"Justin!" Robert whispered to Justin. "Look over there; I think he's trying to hit on your girl, and she looks pretty upset about it."

"What is Blue doing here? And why is he in the trombone section right next to my girlfriend?"

"He joined, apparently, right after school ended last year but couldn't come to sectionals and practices, or so he says."

Justin looked back over to Meganlynn and then at Blue who still had his hand on her hip.

"No, Blue, as far as I'm concerned, you're still the same dirt bag that you always were," she said, removing his hand and then giving him a small pinch of her lips with her eyes focusing right on him. She clenched her fists and a little in her jaw as well. She took in a deep breath and then let it out slowly.

"Oh and what are you going to do about it? Hit me?"

"I don't know." She shook her head and then looked down at the ground. He placed his hand on her leg and then squeezed it a little bit.

"You honestly think that you can defeat me? You're wrong, my girly girl."

"Moron," she stated back, and then they played. Her trombone was shaking since it was right next to his. She needed her personal space and he wasn't giving it to her at all.

"Okay," Mr. Nolls said, stopping for the last time before lunch. Blue hadn't had much time to touch Meganlynn before this, and he had been talking to her less and less. "You all have an hour to eat lunch, relax, and talk to your friends." Then he released them for lunch.

Meganlynn got up, put her trombone in her case, and headed out to talk to her friends. She was very nervous and shaky from her experience. Finally, Justin caught up to her.

"Why were you letting him touch you like that?" Meganlynn looked at Justin with a surprised look in her eyes. Her eyes were starting to fill with tears and her face was quivering with both fear and disgust.

"Let him? Let him! You honestly think that I was letting him do this to me, again?" Her eyes were welling up and tears were starting to form. "Don't hate me," she said, her voice calming down but still sounding teary. "Please, I didn't ask for this to happen to me again. I just—I was just scared that it all was going to happen again. I wanted to be tough and not cry but now look—here I am about to cry in front of you." Justin looked at her and then held out his arms for her to take refuge in. She cried for a minute or two on his shoulder.

When she had finally stopped crying, she stepped back and took a deep breath. Her breath was a bit shaky, but she really couldn't help that part of it. She closed her eyes for a brief second, but all she could possibly see was the picture of Blue trying to feel her up.

"Are you okay?"

Meganlynn nodded and they walked to a lunch table. She took one look at the table that all of Justin's friends were sitting at, and told him that she couldn't possibly sit there.

"I'm going to go over and sit with my friends. Bye."

Justin walked sat down with his friends. He gave Blue a dirty look. "Stay away from her," he told him with the deepest and darkest voice he could possibly have.

"From who?"

"My girlfriend. Who do you think?"

"I didn't think that you guys were going to keep on going out. Seems you two weren't even talking this morning."

"Maybe not, but just stop doing whatever you think you're doing because all that it's doing is scaring her more. She's over there probably crying because you scare her so badly."

"Then good, she should be scared. You have no idea what I plan to do to her."

"I have an idea. Promise that you'll never see the light of day again."

"Yeah, if you can ever catch me."

"Trust me, you do that and I'll find you one way or another, you sick pervert."

"And trust me, Justin, there are other things that are worse than raping her alone."

"Did you guys just hear that?"

"What'd you say?" asked Robert.

"He just said that he'd rape and maybe even do worse things to Meg," answered Justin. "I can't listen to this anymore; I have to go over and sit next to her now." When Justin sat next to Meg, he held her close and kept her close for her safety, every once in a while he would look over to Blue and make sure that he was not anywhere near Meganlynn. After an hour of lunch, they all made their way back into the band room for the remaining of rehearsal.

Once again, Meganlynn sat in her chair, and next to her sat Blue and then John.

"John," Meganlynn said, trying to get John's attention.

"Yeah?" he answered back.

"Can you switch seats with Blue?"

"But Mr. Nolls placed him there personally," he said looking at her with a sad face. "Sorry."

"It's not your fault." Then they began to play again. Blue didn't touch her anymore for the rest of the afternoon.

After they were done playing, the tears had almost dried up in Meganlynn's eyes, and the fear had almost gone from her face. She made her way back over to her case once she was dismissed from their band session.

"You know, you have really pretty eyes," Blue said, looking at the ground. His voice was barley audible because his voice was so low.

"I guess you should know with how much you made them cry and everything."

"I didn't make them cry; you told me that you liked me, and then I started to act on it. You pretty much just shut me off for no reason at all."

"Get away from me."

"I've done nothing wrong. Why should you be mad at me? Shouldn't you be mad at yourself?"

"No, because you have done something wrong, and I'll never forget it, nor will I ever take the blame for everything that you did to me." Then she walked out the door. She yelled good-bye to everyone else and Justin ran after her while she was going to her grandmother's car.

"Meg! Megan! Meganlynn!" he yelled.

"What?" she turned around and asked.

"Please? What did he do now?"

"He was trying to tell me that him harassing me was my fault and that he was never to blame about anything. I told him that I would never believe him about that, that nobody else would believe that I asked for him to harass me, or that I told him that I liked him."

"You wouldn't believe the things that he was saying over at my old lunch table."

"I don't want to hear about them right now. I'm about to leave with my grandmother, and they don't know what happened between Blue and me."

"Okay, well go with them right now before he comes and tries to hurt you again or says anything that will make you even more upset. I love you." Then he hugged her tight, and she left the building and got into the car with her grandmother. She was finally safe without anybody to mess it up.

"Did you have fun?" her grandmother asked her as soon as she got into the car.

"Yeah, I had fun," she answered back.

CHAPTER 2

Finally, the next day had come, and Meganlynn had spent the whole night studying since she couldn't get any sleep at all. She had thought a lot about all of the things that he had done to her, and got so upset that she actually wrote in her diary. Frankly, she was too scared to even think about going back to band camp, let alone to even think about Justin or any of her friends that she wanted to tell. She didn't know how to tell them other than to walk up behind them and be like: "So guess who's getting harassed again? And guess by whom again!" She couldn't bring herself to do it, though. She wanted greatly to tell her god-brother, Jacob, but he would probably kill Blue and then go to jail.

Her mother went into the car, and Meganlynn followed close behind her. She didn't want her mother to be late just because she didn't want to go to band camp. Her mother dropped her off at her grandmother's house. Her aunt was awake and greeted her as she walked through the door.

"Hey, Meg," she said.

"Hey, Aunt Holly," Meganlynn replied.

"Wowie! Look at those sexy legs!"

Meganlynn turned slowly around. She had said it again. Meganlynn then ran into the living room, and she didn't come back out until it was time to go to band camp.

On the way to band camp, her grandmother and aunt stumbled over her *sexy legs*. Unfortunately, though, she had no other choice than to listen to this and to just deal with it. Finally they arrived at the middle school and Meganlynn finally felt that she was free.

With her face red and her hands shaking, she walked to the back of the van and took her trombone out of the car.

"What's bothering you so much that your face is so red?" asked her aunt. Meganlynn didn't really feel like answering, and she didn't feel as though they deserved any answers from her. She shut the door in her face and walked off toward the school.

"Meg! Give me an answer now! I'll tell your father!" yelled her aunt after her.

Go right ahead and tell my father! All I actually have to do is tell him that you have been calling me "sexy legs" again, and I promise you that he'll understand! she thought to herself. Her aunt then got out of the car and followed her inside. She was a couple of seconds behind her, but she caught up to her when Meganlynn was getting her trombone out.

"Meganlynn, you don't ever walk away from me! We are your elders! Do you understand me, young lady?" she yelled at the top of her lungs.

"Aunt Holly, you're making a scene," Meg answered, walking back to her section.

"Why are you shouting at her in here?" asked Lily Brown, or as the other band students knew her, Mrs.

Brown. She was Justin's mother, and she and Meganlynn had met earlier in the year.

"She doesn't have any respect for anybody! She's out there having sex with every guy she sees! I bet you one hundred and fifty dollars that she has cheated on Justin over there at least sixty times in the past week, and I don't just mean kissing cheating, I mean banging cheating! She's such a little slut that she can't even keep a guy for a day! You know, Justin's stupid for even staying with her because she has banged her god brother at least sixteen times in the past three months, and they tell me that I was a pot head! I was nothing compared to her! She does every kind of drug that there is possible! And I used to drink? No! Not me. Compared to her I was a saint! You or somebody needs to teach her some manners like this!" Then she slapped her niece as hard and as fast as she could across the face. Her niece fell to the ground.

"Ma'am," Lily said, standing between Meganlynn and her aunt. "That was my son that you were calling stupid for sticking with her! By the way, she was always very nice and polite whenever I was around her so why don't you try to get to know the real Meganlynn that everybody else knows. And one more thing," she said while all of Meganlynn's friends were starting to gather around.

"What?" Aunt Holly spat back at Mrs. Morgan.

"I think you made the entire band very angry with you," she answered.

"Fine, I'll go. You, little brat—you better be out there at three o'clock sharp!" She walked back to the car after hitting her niece for the last time.

"Good thing I didn't bring my computer here today," she said to Justin as he was helping her up.

"Come here," Mrs. Morgan said to Meganlynn, taking her back to Mr. Nolls's office. "What was that all about?"

"Well they used to call me 'sexy legs' when I was eight, and they were calling me it again this morning. They were just being total jerks. Then, my Aunt Holly came in and made a whole scene about it."

"So they were just being jerks, okay then, we'll call your dad, tell him what went on, and see what he wants us to do. You're not going to go home with your grandma and aunt. Go ahead and go out there and play. I'll call your father."

"Thank you," answered Meganlynn. Then she left the room and went into the band room and sat in her seat right next to Blue.

"Hey there, sexy," Blue said to her as he was going to sit down.

"Stop calling me whatever, and stop doing whatever because your sexual harassments are just getting a little bit old, so just stop."

"Never," he whispered in her ear before they began to play. "Never will I stop." Then they played the music that was in front of them. Tears slowly ran from Meganlynn's eyes as they played the many pieces.

"What are you crying for?" asked Mr. Nolls when he came over to look at the trombones.

"I'm not," she said in her shaky voice. "My eyes are just watering."

Justin looked at her with his glaring look.

Why didn't she tell him the truth? Justin wondered to himself. *I mean, if she ever wants this to end, then why didn't she tell Mr. Nolls what Blue was doing to her? She needs to tell him. Maybe she wants me, as her boyfriend, to stick up for her before she tells, or maybe she's just too scared to say anything. I have absolutely no idea, but we have at least another five minutes until our hour lunch break, so I'll ask her then.* The five minutes went by surprisingly quickly for him, but not for Meganlynn.

For the next five minutes, Meganlynn was tortured. Mr. Nolls had stopped the band to give them some more time to get their strength back. When Mr. Nolls wasn't looking, Blue decided that he was going to touch Meganlynn again. He then put his hand on her hip and then slid his hand down her leg. He leaned in and tried to kiss but she turned her face away looking at Justin with a tearful glint in her eyes. She had no idea that he was watching the whole time.

That's going to take a long time for her to get over, thought Justin to himself looking at the trombone section.

"Keep your filthy hands off of me," she whispered to Blue.

"What do you think that I want to do? Just say things to you?"

"No, I don't even want to know what you want to do to me. But just keep—your—your hand out of my pants." Meganlynn told him, leaning against Justin.

Justin then wrapped his arms around her and placed his head on her shoulder. Meganlynn was almost crying while she watched Blue walk out of the door.

"Okay, you all are dismissed for lunch, have fun. You have one hour," Mr. Nolls said. Then everyone got up and left.

"Okay, let's go out there, get our lunch, and then go outside where he won't find us."

"It sounds like a plan," she replied as they walked out the door with Justin's arm around her waist. They went into the lunch room and sat down at the table that Meganlynn's friends were all at. Justin then took Meganlynn and all of her friends back to the outside of the school and up toward the bottom baseball field. They had about forty minutes left until they had to be back at the football field.

"So now that you are already upset, can I ask you a question about eighth grade?"

"Why not? I'm remembering it all anyway."

"What did Blue do to you the first time he did this to you?"

"He did a lot."

"As in?"

"Should I tell him?" Meganlynn asked her friends.

"Yeah, you really should. He did ask. Aren't you the one who said if he would ask you, then you would definitely tell him everything that happened?" asked Lizzie.

"Yeah, I guess I did say that." Meg turned back to Justin. "Can you stand tears if I start crying?"

"Yes, just tell me all of it so I know. I was with you when you were going through all of this the first time; I deserve to know."

"Fine." She took a deep breath. "It all started on the day that I had left for Youth Retreat in eighth grade. He had been trying to pass notes with me. I told him that I didn't pass notes, so he made them simple yes or no questions. He started off with *do you have a boyfriend?* and I told him that I did. He then asked me who it was, and I told him that it was you.

"About two weeks later, he told me that I was in his group for science class. I knew that he liked me, but I didn't think he would go to such extremes as to show me he liked me. He then began saying crude things to me. He looked at Jessie Wingly and said, 'Watch this, I can creep her out in just one second.' Then, he turned to me and said, 'I can see everything from here.' He was staring at my butt while saying this. I then turned away and crisscrossed my arms so that they covered my stomach. It made me feel better. I was still offended, but I didn't think anything of it, even though I should have.

"Then he would say some stuff that I don't really want to repeat, all of it was crude and inappropriate.

"The next day, he explained all of the things that he had imagined doing to me, and then he asked me if I wanted to join in." Meg's voice was scratchy and more worried than normal at this point as though she was on the verge of crying, and she was. She had to get it all out though. She felt as though she owed it to Justin to tell him everything that went on between them. "By this time, I was feeling more offended and weirded-out by his behavior. I just wanted him away from me. I felt—how do I put this?—dirty.

"After that, he came on much, much stronger. He decided I should be with him instead of with you, even though I wanted to be with you because I actually love you. I was sitting all huddled up in my chair and a colored pencil that I was drawing with, happened to make a mark on my face. Well, Blue and his friends were explaining something to me, and by this time, I basally hated him and wanted him gone. I looked at him and then started to reach for my face. As I was reaching for it, he told me, 'No, let me get that.' Then he grabbed my face and started to stroke my face. He had this twisted smile on his face, and I was scared that the teacher was going to bust us for PDA. If I was going to get caught for PDA with anybody, then it was going to be you and not him. I didn't exactly think 'Keep your hands off my stinkin' face!' was going to work since he never listened to me anyway. I slapped his hand so hard that he was shaking his hand in pain. I wish that I would've kept on going and just beat the living crap out of him, but I was so scared and felt so belittled that it wouldn't have mattered anyway. I wanted you more than anything, and I always looked forward to the band classes where you would be there to protect me. It was everything that kept me sane. Don't you think the idea of 'I don't like you, so stay away,' would get through to him? But no, not Blue; he's too stupid to figure anything out. So he decided that I was in need of a break for a few days, and I thought that he was done with all of his harassment crap. But no, not Blue.

"Then, at the start of the next week, he decided that he wanted to go all sexy on me. I was horrible at math by this point. I couldn't pay attention to anything in class besides him and trying to focus all of my hatred on him. But then,

I was standing in line for lunch, and like I said, he decided to go all sexy on me and try to make me like him even more. He walked up behind me and whispered the words, 'Hey, there sexy' in my ear so that I would jump. I didn't turn around because I already knew that it was him, and I didn't want him to kiss me.

"Well, from that day on, he didn't stop describing his fantasies and asking me to join in, nor did he stop poking me in my sides. I was so annoyed with everything, every time that he would ever do anything to me that, given the chance, I would've switched schools. But since I apparently like to show-up the people who put me down, I didn't. The other reason I didn't move is because of all of my friends and you.

"Well, about a week after continually doing all of this to me, he decided that it was time for a little bit of hand holding. He tried to hold hands with me, even though I wanted nothing to do with it. I had my hand a little bit outside of his reach, and he put his hand on top of mine. I would move my hand, and then he would move his so it was on top of my hand once again. We did this for about three minutes until I finally moved my hand out of the way so much that he couldn't reach it with his hand. While he was doing this, he would look at me with this strange look on his face as if he was asking, 'do you like me now?' I wanted to scream something that would get the teacher's attention, but I was way too scared to even start to think about screaming. The scream itself would've only come out as a whisper anyway." Meganlynn started crying on Justin's shoulder.

"I think we should probably start heading back," Justin then told the girls, holding Meganlynn. He patted her back and reminded her that he was there. His face was full of rage and frustration, but his touch was still warm towards Meganlynn. He had no idea what to do, so he just held her to show that she was safe in his arms.

"Why? We still have a half hour Justin," stated Lizzie.

"But I think that I can hear thunder, and they'll want everybody in for this."

"Good point." They all got back up and went back into the band room.

"What was that for?" she asked him.

"That's to make up for the kiss that Blue gave you."

"No, the one that has to make up for Blue's kiss has to be big."

"I have a lot of kissing to do then."

"Yeah, and you can't tell me that you won't like it."

"You're right; I honestly can't tell you that."

"I love you," Meganlynn told him with a smile on her face.

"I love you, too," he replied, kissing her again. Then they walked the rest of the way back into the band room.

When the lunch break was almost over, Mr. Nolls went into his office to check the weather and see what was going on because the wind was blowing so hard that a couple of the branches had fallen off some nearby trees. Meanwhile, the band didn't have to play.

"Band," Mr. Nolls said. "Put your instruments away and follow me when you're done. We are going to go and find a place to wait out this tornado."

Justin leaned forward and began to kiss Meganlynn and hold her safe. Blue slowly began to pull on her while Justin had his grip upon her. She let go of Justin's lips and began to move closer to Justin and out of Blue's reach.

"What's wrong?" Justin asked, whispering in her ear.

"What do you think is wrong? Blue's right here, sitting next to me," she replied.

Justin moved Meganlynn from the side that Blue was sitting on to the side that had her other friends on it. Justin then put his arms back around Meganlynn and started to kiss her once again.

Meganlynn was trying to get away from all of her hurtful memories that had happened that day, and Justin was trying to get Meganlynn away from everything that had happened to her that day. She needed an escape and he was willing to give it to her.

They still sat there looking at each other and then kissed once before leaning back. Meganlynn had tears slowly running down her face. She wasn't scared about the tornado that was apparently coming, but she was scared about Blue and what he was going to do to her. She could only be around Justin so much; Justin played the tuba and she played the trombone.

"Mr. Nolls," started one of the percussionists named Ashley.

"Yes?" he answered back.

"How long are we going to stay down here?"

"Well, the warning goes until six o'clock so I'm going to have to say until six fifteen."

Blue came up to Meganlynn and Justin. She was so disgusted with him that she broke off the kiss.

"What's wrong?" Justin whispered in her ear, worrying that Blue was around her again.

"Blue's here," she whispered back.

"Why does he always have to come around you?" he whispered, and then he looked back to see Blue behind her. "Who's over here?" Justin asked feeling around the floor.

"Lizzie," Lizzie answered.

"Meganlynn's going to come to you for a little visit," he whispered and then placed Meganlynn on his lap, then he placed Meganlynn on the other side of him. He had his arm around her waist. Meganlynn was crying now more than ever.

The time flew by, and Blue didn't try anything else for the rest of the time since he really couldn't get to Meganlynn through the blockade of girls and Justin. Around four, Meganlynn went into a daydream, and Justin was all alone to worry about her issues by himself. At six, they opened the door, and then they were free to go home.

"Meganlynn," Justin whispered in her ear, but she didn't come out of it. He checked her wrist for a pulse, and there was one, but she was totally and completely gone. He knew that she wasn't going to wake, so he picked her up and walked out the door with Mr. Nolls giving him a very weird look.

"Justin, is she dead?" Mr. Nolls asked Justin.

"No, she's just in a really deep sleep," he answered and then took her over by her friends.

Blue saw that she wasn't completely there and saw an opportunity to take her away from Justin and into his own clutches. He snuck more and more toward Meganlynn. She woke and saw him coming for her.

"Justin," she said pointing over at Blue.

"What?" Then he saw Blue. "Can you stand up?" he asked and then set her back on the ground. He walked over to Blue.

"Hi, Justin I was just seeing if Meganlynn was okay."

"Yeah, since when can I ever believe anything that you say?"

"Since now."

"Try never. Now turn around and go the other way."

"Why should I?"

"Because if you don't, I'll go and tell Mr. Nolls that you can't seem to keep your hands off of my girlfriend."

"You do that, and she'll be dead before sunrise tomorrow."

"Stay away from her."

"No. Let's try that answer." Blue walked past him and right toward Meganlynn. Justin turned and punched him as hard as he could.

"What do you think about that response?"

"Try taking it back, and I'll think about not raping your girlfriend, okay?"

"You lay one more hand on her, and before you know it, the police will be back at the scene, and you'll be going to jail," he walked back to Meganlynn and placed her in his arms again.

"Meganlynn," said a voice. It was Lily.

"Yeah?" she answered.

"Your dad's here to pick you up and take you home."

"Okay, thanks." She then hugged all of her friends good-bye and walked over to get her things. Blue was standing right by her trombone. She gave him a very pathetic look. "Will you please just let me by?"

"Never."

"Let her get her stuff," said the commanding voice of Meganlynn's father.

"Why should I listen to you?"

"I'm her father, and I can absolutely promise you that I know everything that you have been doing to her."

"Fine, here's your stuff," he said, handing Meganlynn her things. He then took her trombone, opened the case, and licked the mouthpiece all over. "Now you can kiss me whenever you play whether you like it or not."

"You are one sick little kid, and that is not normal. I hope that you can either get help or go to jail before you touch my daughter again!" he shouted trying to keep himself back from completely trying to kill him.

Justin walked her back to her car while her father followed close behind in case Blue got any other ideas on what to do to Meganlynn while she was still there. Her father wasn't about to let her out of his sight until he was sure that she was safe in someone's arms. They finally got to her car, and he gave her a hug, opened the door, watched her put her trombone in the back, and then gave her another hug.

"Do you know how much new mouthpieces are?" her father asked.

"No, but I'll call you later and tell you."

"Okay."

"I love you."

"Love you, too."

He did call her later that night and she was still crying over everything that had happened throughout the day. He told her that a new mouthpiece was twenty dollars, and that Mr. Nolls had one more in stock. He told her that he loved her and then asked if he could go to church with her on Sunday. She asked her parents, and they said he could. They both were happy.

"See you on Sunday. Love you." He ended the phone call.

"Love you too, and I can't wait." They hung up, and Meganlynn finally relaxed, thinking she didn't need to worry about Blue for the rest of the weekend.

CHAPTER 3

Sunday came quickly, and before Meganlynn knew it, she was running in her high heels trying to get her makeup on to look pretty for Justin. She knew that she wasn't going to look all that pretty for him once she was in band camp. She missed him more than anybody at band, and he missed her more than anybody at school, period. Meganlynn waited and waited for the car to finally pull down his road and then into his driveway.

"Hello," said Lily to Meganlynn as she walked over to Meganlynn's car.

"Hi," said Meganlynn back as she walked over to Justin.

"Hey, sweetie," answered Justin, looking at his girlfriend. She had changed since he had last seen her. She now was wearing a black hooded jacket and shirt, dark jeans, and dark make-up. The only thing that Blue wasn't able to take away from her was the fact that she was still wearing her high heels. They may have been black, but they were still high heels. He hadn't taken away her religion from her either. Justin looked at her kind of weirdly and wondered why she was wearing a black hooded jacket in the middle of summer.

"Why are you looking at me like that?" Meganlynn asked after he had been looking at her for a few seconds.

"You look so—" He had to stop and think for a moment to figure out how to say it without offending her. He knew that she needed him now more than anything, especially right now. "You look so, so...black."

"What's that supposed to mean?" Her eyebrow was raised a little. *What was Justin going to do about Blue?*

"Nothing bad, but you're wearing so much black."

"Yeah, I'm cold, and I want more sunlight to come to me."

"Yeah right, you're wearing all of this because of Blue, aren't you?"

"No, I would never let him control me!"

"Well, guess what? By making you wear all of that black, he is controlling you!"

"He's not controlling me, don't worry about it."

"I can't help but worry for you."

"I know, and I'm trying to tell you to stop caring about it. Don't worry that he's controlling my life, because he's not."

"As long as he's not, and he's keeping his hands off you."

"Well, at least my friends can't say that you're not worried about me, because you obviously are."

"Has he touched you since the last day of band practice?"

"I haven't seen him since the last day, thankfully."

"If you see him outside of band and school, you just stay away from him, you understand?"

"Yes, sir!"

"Nice to see that you have your sense of humor back."

"Only until tomorrow."

"How long am I staying with you?"

"Church, and then we're going to dinner with our parents."

"Oh, yeah, so you can tell me everything that's been going on with him."

"I'll tell you when I tell Nerverah," she answered him. Nerverah was her best friend from her church that was a lot like Meganlynn herself. She was the person that Meganlynn would run to whenever she was dealing with issues with Blue beforehand.

"Will you tell her every little detail?"

"Well, I'll try to, but whatever I don't get to tell you there, I'll tell you whenever I can. You're going to see a lot of tears shed from my eyes."

"I'll be there to hold you every step of the way, I promise."

"Thank you," she said as a small tear came to her eye.

"Why wouldn't I?"

"I don't know. I guess you wouldn't if you didn't believe me."

"I didn't want to at first, but when he kissed you, and you were just looking at me, I knew that you were going through torture, and that you had absolutely no desire to be with him."

"Trust me, I have absolutely no intention of being with any part of him."

"I know, and that's why you and I are still together. In fact, if I had any idea that you liked him more than you like me, then we would be done before he was even done kissing you yesterday."

"Why does he want to hurt me like this?"

"Probably because you are beautiful, smart, wonderful, and—did I mention beautiful?"

"Yes, and thank you for those compliments."

"You're so welcome, but only because you deserve them."

"And if I didn't?"

"Well…"

"Okay, I get the point," she said with a smile on her face. "We should probably head back to the car now, church will be starting soon."

"Okay, come on then." With a simple 'bye' from Justin's mother, they were all off to have a relaxing day at church, and then off to have dinner with their parents.

Finally, when they arrived at the church, they walked in. Meganlynn and Justin went up to the youth room and sat down. They talked about random things that had happened to them and had a sort of normal conversation. Class was just about to start when the assistant pastor walked into the youth room with another person right behind her.

"Meganlynn," she started. "This is Blue Robenson. He is a visitor and he doesn't have anyone to sit next to or to show him around. Could you show him around?"

"I guess I—"

"Good, then I will see you all downstairs for the church service. Good-bye."

"Well hello there, Meganlynn," Blue said while touching her hair just lightly enough to feel it.

"Get away from me."

"But you agreed to show me around."

"Fine, what do you want to see?"

"Well, I've seen everything that I came here to see."

"Okay, then leave, now."

"Naw, I don't think I will. I think I'll stay and listen to what you call 'God's Word.'"

"Why don't you just leave me alone and find someone else to harass?"

"But Meganlynn…Don't you see? You and I are supposed to be together. You need to realize this; it's fate."

"Okay, let me make one thing clear," said Nerverah as she stood up. "One, you and Meganlynn will never be together because A, she loves someone else, and B, she hates you. Two, you will never be together because it's not God's will."

"How do you know that it's not God's will, you little blonde?"

"She's not blonde, and does a rapist ever marry his prey? No. Do they ever date? No. Do they ever fall in love? No. Does she really want to remember all the memories that she can now see in her mind! You and I are never going to be together!" Meganlynn screamed at the top of her lungs hoping that Blue would actually understand some of what she was saying.

"Are you ever going to get a mind of your own? I'm the one who needs to get my figures straight and you're the one that's telling me this. You're the one who fantasized about me sexually harassing you. You fantasized about it so much that you told on me for something that I didn't do!"

"If you didn't do it then why did you admit to it?" Her voice was back to being calm, but she was crying harder than anybody had ever seen her cry. Justin had his arms around her waist, trying to hold her back from what she might do. Blue proceeded to yell and move closer and closer to her.

"I just figured it would be a whole lot easier."

"Because you did it to me! This time and the time before!" She couldn't help but scream now. She had to, there wasn't any other way that the words could get out.

"I didn't do this to you, honey, you wanted me to do that to you. You asked me to."

"How on earth would she ask you to do that to her?" asked Justin.

"By her beautiful eyes."

"Shut up!" she screamed back to Blue.

"No!" he screamed, running his hand across her face. The mark that his hand had left was one that was hard and bruised. "You need to have a little bit of a memory of what happened when I asked you out," he whispered in her ear.

"I do I remember exactly what happened," she spoke in a low voice as she got up and walked out of the youth room.

"Get your act together man. I wouldn't be surprised if she was cheating on you with that red-head right there."

"You did that to her. When you were doing it, she didn't tell me because she wanted her boyfriend more than anything; she needed me. She needed me there with her. She felt protected by me, not by you. I saw the look of hurt in her eyes, and I saw her shake. I felt her shake whenever I was holding her. She was terrified! You made her that way," Justin said now, rushing back out of the door of the youth room along with Nerverah by his side.

Once he found his way to the sanctuary, he walked through the doors and found Meganlynn sitting with her mother and father, talking to them.

"We have to leave," she begged and pleaded with her parents.

"Honey, why?" her mother asked her.

"Bl—" She cried and cried, but she couldn't spit the name out.

"Blue's here," Justin filled in for her, sitting behind her and rubbing her back.

"Honey, find someone else to do the ushering. We're leaving," Meganlynn's mother told her father.

"Okay." Then Meganlynn's father got up and left. Meganlynn and her mother left with Justin following closely behind her.

"I'm sorry," Meganlynn said, crying in her hands and then crying on Justin's shoulder.

"Honey, it's not your fault," her mother said.

"Yes it is; everything is. He just keeps on coming back and back and following me wherever I go. I'm so, so, so sick of being stalked and followed and feeling as though this is my fault! I want to feel normal again. But I can't because in order to feel that way, I have to have him—" She left off to breathe heavily for a few seconds. "I have to have him leave me alone for good. I can't get a restraining order, because there isn't enough evidence, I can't get him arrested either because he would never admit to it again."

"Meganlynn," Justin whispered in her ear. "None of this is your fault. He's just an idiot that apparently can't live without you. He isn't going to rape you or do anything else to you like he keeps on claiming. This isn't your fault, it's his fault."

"But everything he keeps on saying—"

"Forget about it. He doesn't know the first thing about you. I knew more about you the first day I met you than he knows about you now."

"Yeah, but—I mean—still. Justin, he's here. He's at my church. I feel as though I'm letting someone down, when really I'm not."

"Shh," he said, pulling her close to his chest trying to comfort her. Meganlynn's father then started the car and drove away. Meganlynn settled down a little bit more and then started to relax. She had calmed down, and everything seemed to be a little bit easier for her to comprehend. She had to forget all about it and have fun with her parents and her boyfriend, no matter what she was forgetting.

"What do you want to do now that we've played hooky from church for the day?" Meganlynn's mother asked her.

"I don't know. You guys pick something," Meganlynn answered. She still sounded like she was about to cry.

"Let's go to the mall and have some fun at least. The mall is having one of those huge Early Bird specials that they throw every year," her mother told her father, and then she turned so that she was in view of both Meganlynn and Justin. "Is that okay with you Justin?" she asked him.

"Yeah, as long as she gets better than she is right now," he answered, holding his girlfriend close to him.

"She will be," her father assured him.

When they had arrived at the mall, Meganlynn's phone started to ring. Meganlynn still looked pretty upset, and she didn't recognize the number that was coming up from the phone, and just in case it was Blue, she had her mother answer it.

"Hello," her mother answered.

"Dad," Meganlynn said.

"Yes, honey," he answered

"I'm going to go into that store," Meganlynn told her father pointing over toward one of the clothing stores that was across the hallway. Her father nodded his head, and she was off.

"Aren't you going to follow her?" her father asked Justin.

"Sir, she's going into an underwear store, and I really don't want to go into that store."

"I understand, but you may have to go and get her out of there. Her mother is coming over here, and she looks very happy."

"Huh, wonder what is the matter with her."

"I don't think anything is wrong with her, but boy, she looks happier than earlier today."

"Yeah, you got that right." By the time Justin and Mr. VanDeritie conversation was over, Meganlynn's mother had returned.

"Great news! That phone number that just called was a publisher! They want to publish her book! Someone finally responded! This is going to cheer up her day so much!" answered Mrs. VanDeritie, who then jumped up and down because she was so happy for her daughter.

"Justin, why don't you go and get Meganlynn for us?"

"Yes sir," he said, going into the store.

I wonder if this means that she's going to be leaving me for some big movie actor or something. I hope that she can stay and that she won't leave me, he thought to himself. By the time he had gotten to Meganlynn, he saw the grim look on her face, and she was shaking in her skin. He wanted nothing more than to just go on up there and make her laugh so loud that mall security would have to kick them both out for disturbing the peace.

"Meg," he said quietly walking up to her.

"I should've known that you would've followed me in here. I should've known!" she said turning around with a high-heel in her hand that had the sharpness of a dagger.

"Meganlynn! It's me! Your boyfriend! Justin!"

"Oh! Justin, I'm so sorry! Please forgive me. I thought that you were Blue."

"I know."

"Not that you look anything like Blue at all, it's just that, I'm so paranoid that nothing seems like everything to me."

"I know," he said, pulling her into an embrace in his arms.

"What did you come in here for, anyway?" she asked him.

"I wanted to make sure that you were all right," he said, smiling.

"Yeah, right. I'll be right out, just let me buy these things."

"What are they?"

"Justin, they're body lotions."

"Oh, sorry."

"It's okay," she said, smiling. She walked up to the cash register while he walked out of the door and back to Meganlynn's parents.

"Where is she?" her father asked.

"She'll be right out. She had to buy something."

"Okay, but the news is just so exciting!" squealed her mother. They waited for about five minutes. Her mother was wearing a never-ending smile that nothing could possibly break. "Hi, honey!" her mother yelled, making Meganlynn jump back.

"Mom, are you on a sugar high?"

"You'll be like this too once you hear my news!"

"What could possibly make me like that?"

"Your book is going to be published!" her mother screamed, making everyone jump back a couple of steps. Meganlynn stood there with her eyes open wide and her heart about ready to burst out of her chest. She looked over at her father and at Justin with her eyes so big that he couldn't help but laugh.

"Is she kidding?" she asked them. Justin and her father both shook their heads. Her eyes got wider, and then she jumped up and back down again after she had taken in the news for a few seconds. "My book is getting published!" she shouted, jumping up and down for a second and then breathing heavily.

"Want to go and get a dress?" her mother asked.

"Are you guys paying for it?"

"Of course."

"Shoes and accessories?"

"As long as they're not pure diamond or pure gold or cost a lot of money," her father stepped in.

"Fine."

"What would you like, though?" her father asked.

"Justin, you take her dress shopping and tell her the truth about how the dress looks on her. Help her shop for accessories and shoes as well," she told Justin. "Do you have your debit card on you?" she asked, turning to Meganlynn's father.

"Yes," he answered.

"Okay, Meganlynn, do you have a problem with that?"

"Are you kidding? Shopping for an expensive dress that I want and love? Hmm, should I have a problem with that?"

"No. So since we are meeting Justin's parents at one o'clock, we better meet you guys back here at twelve thirty. See you then. Oh! If you need us, just call our cell phones."

"Okay," said both Meganlynn and Justin, walking away from her parents and toward the famous dress shop that was right at the end of the mall. Justin had a strange feeling and told himself not to leave Meganlynn's side all afternoon. Even if she had to go to the bathroom, he would go and stand by the doorway, because he knew deep down inside of him that there was a predator trying to catch his prey.

Yes, he knew that Blue was there with both of them while they were alone together. He could have made them walk back to her parents, and everything would've been all right even if he did not get to kiss her in every dress that she tried on. He did not want to ruin his special day with Meganlynn, though, so he vowed to stay next to her and protect her. They then turned and walked into the dress shop.

"What about this one?" Meganlynn asked Justin. She was wearing a floor-length, green and purple dress that pooled out at the bottom with a frail tulle material around the skirt of the dress. The top was actually a dull shade of yellow and had very, very bright purple sparkles sprinkled all over it. The straps that came off of the top of the dress were a very deep blue that everyone would like, but were also the type of color that no one would possibly want to see on that dress.

"No, I don't think so," he said, stepping back away from her. He looked the dress up and down again. Meganlynn then walked over to her purse and took out her camera.

"Here, let's get a picture," she said while he held her close. She then held the camera up and got a picture of the two of them together. "Justin, here take my picture alone," she said giving her camera over to him.

"Okay," he said, holding the camera up so she could pose for it. She leaned up against a chair and then puckered up her lips. "That was a good one," Justin said laughing at it.

"Oh, really?" Meganlynn asked, walking over to the camera so she could also see the picture. "Oh, yeah that's totally the right picture to send to all of my family members." She laughed.

"Let's not get your whole family involved, let's just keep this between our parents and some friends, okay?"

"Well, fine." She breathed heavily and then laughed. She was having the time of her life, but the one person that she didn't want there was there even if she didn't notice him.

"Go, try on another dress," he said, laughing at her back.

"Okay," she said, walking away to go and find another dress, though she was still in the dress that was completely ugly on her. Now, it was time for some serious dress shopping. Then, she scurried back to the dressing room to try on another dress.

This time, when she came out of the dressing room, her dress flowed past the floor and onto the ground way past her feet. The dress was red and had fake diamonds on the line of the dress that was toward her neckline. The waistline had the same sparkles but on an optional belt. There weren't any sleeves on it, and the bottom lining of it was decorated with the same sort of fake diamonds that the belt and the neckline had. There was also a small slit in the side of the dress. The slit was a very light pink that almost looked as though it was white. Meganlynn looked as though she was a princess, and she looked very beautiful in this dress.

"The dress is too long," she whispered to Justin.

"If you get that dress, you could just get a very high pair of heels." He smiled at her.

"So, what do you think about it?"

"Well, I don't know; let's see how you kiss in it." He leaned forward to kiss her. He touched her lips very softly, and before Meganlynn knew it, she was in his arms and pressed up against his chest. She missed him, and she needed him. She still didn't know that Blue was right behind her, and that he was stalking her all over the mall.

If she didn't know, then she didn't care. If he was following her all over the place, she didn't have a clue about it since she was so excited about her book being published.

"So?" she asked Justin as he pulled away. He still held her in his arms.

"I think this could be the dress."

"Really?"

"Well you kiss well and look good in it."

"Still, I want to look fabulous," she said, fanning out her arms and acting like a showgirl with her hip cocked and her feet hidden by the foot of the skirt of the dress.

"You do."

"Not in jeans."

"No. You still do no matter what you wear."

"Well, still. I have to be the prettiest person there."

"Why are you worrying about your looks so much?"

"This is my book, and I am getting my book published finally. I need to be the prettiest person there!" She had a smile on her face. Justin tried hard not to imagine the girl he would have to hold if she knew that Blue was right behind them, watching her every time she came out of the dressing room. He didn't want to tell her, but a very tiny part of him still wanted to have her sad, because she was usually in his arms when she was sad. He wanted to hold her in his arms forevermore and never have anyone else hold her. He knew that it was only a matter of time before she would find someone else in the publishing world that was probably a whole lot cuter than he was, and who was probably a whole lot nicer than he was. He would miss her and didn't want her book to get published for that reason.

"You don't have to be the prettiest person there because you will already be the star for getting your book published."

"Yeah, but along with being the star, you are the center of attention and the person that everyone looks at. So, with everyone looking at you, you naturally want to look good in your dress."

"But you don't need a dress to look good."

"Maybe not, but this is still an extremely formal party that I'm throwing, and I want to look nice."

"Fine," he said, holding up the camera once again. They took a picture and then took one of just Meganlynn sitting down in a chair and looking up at the sky as if she was wondering what was going to happen the next day.

"That was a really good one," whispered Justin, looking at the picture. "You do know that you could be a model, right?"

"Yeah, I know, but I love writing even more. I mean, sure it would be cool to be a model, but the girly-girl aspect just isn't me."

"I'd buy every magazine that you were in if you were one."

"I'm sure a lot of people would, and that a lot of guys would make that promise and keep it."

"This one will never let you down though."

"Fine, you win."

"Thank you," Justin answered, smiling at her.

"You're welcome." They looked at one another for a few seconds. Justin took her in his arms and held her for a few minutes.

"Yeah, I think this could be the dress."

"Are you sure?"

"Yes."

"Okay, but let me try on one other dress before you say anything about this one."

"Fine."

"Okay, let me pick out some more. What time is it?"

"10:50," he answered.

"Okay, so we'll pick our favorite out of all of them and then go and get the rest of the stuff."

"Sounds good to me."

"Okay," she said, stepping out of the dressing room. This dress was also floor-length and had a crisscross in the front. The neckline was a v-neck, and the back was open. The dress had a halter top, fake diamonds, and fake blue and pink sapphires on it. The crisscross in the front had the added beauty of having a little cross in the front made out of lab-created sapphires with lab-created pink sapphires all around the border of the cross. Where the crisscross would've touched even more material, the dress had an open back and had the material coming to her lower back.

"Now, we have to get a picture of this one."

"Okay," she said, poising her stance with tennis shoes in her hands while wearing a white, flowing, beautiful dress. She looked as innocent as she could, and it was by far the best picture of her that they had taken all day. Justin looked at the picture, and he wanted a copy of it just in case she decided that he wasn't good enough because he wasn't rich and famous.

"Can I have a copy of this one?" he asked her, holding the camera up so she could see the picture that he wanted.

"Can you have a copy?" she asked, smiling. "What do you think I am, a model?" She swayed back and forth. "Of course you can have a copy of this picture."

"Thanks," he said, kissing her on the lips. He then held the camera and snapped a picture of the two of them.

"Well, I guess I like this one the best."

"Me too."

"Yeah," she said back. Then she turned around and went into the dressing room once again to change her clothes. She finally came out wearing her normal clothes and her tennis shoes on her feet instead of in her hands. He looked at the picture again and then looked at the pictures of the both of them and smiled. If she really ever did leave him, he would miss her more than she would ever know.

"Let's pay for this," she said then walked to the cash register. Justin followed closely behind her, his hand around her waist in hopes that she would stay if he was touching her. She looked up at the people once again and then back at him.

"Look! The new makeup store. Let's go in there."

"I'm going to be out here, okay?"

"Yeah, I'll only be a half-hour."

"Better be quicker than that; we only have an hour before we have to meet our parents."

"Fine," she thought for a minute or two. "Ten minutes."

"Okay, I'll see you then."

"Fine." Then Justin kissed her once again and went out to the bench and sat down. She went into the makeup store. Once she had finally walked into the makeup store, he went into the jewelry store to get her something as well. He was proud of her, and he also wanted her to have something to remember him by if she ever had to move or go someplace.

"Hello, sir," said the cashier. There wasn't anyone in the store at the moment.

"Hey," he said back.

"Can I help you with something?"

"I'm looking for something for my girlfriend. She just got her book published, and I want to get her something nice to remember me by if she ever has to go away."

"Okay, what does she like?"

"She likes writing, crosses, animals, four-wheeling, and hearts—the shape not the thing in your chest."

"Look at this necklace right here; it also comes with a matching ring for free." He took a necklace shaped like a cross out of the cabinet. It had a sapphire heart in the middle of it. The cross was gold with a diamond in each of the four ends of the cross.

"Can I look at the ring?"

"Yes, it's right here," the cashier said, opening the cabinet once again to take out the most dazzling ring that Justin had ever seen in his life. The ring had sapphire heart outline with a diamond cross in the center of it.

"Hold the ring up to the light and read what it says. She is a Christian, right?" asked the salesman.

"Yes, she is," Justin answered, holding the ring up to the light. In it, you could see the writing that read: *The Lord is my Shepherd. Yeah, though I walk through the valley of darkness, I shall fear no evil for the Lord is my Shepherd.*

"What do you think of it?"

"I love it and so will she."

"So, are you going to get it?"

"Let me make one quick phone call."

After confirming her ring size with her mother, Justin hung up the phone.

"Are you getting it?" asked the cashier excitedly.

"How much is it?"

"Seems you caught us at eighty-percent off on our already on-sale prices so… probably around two hundred dollars. We're having a huge markdown because we're closing our doors."

"I'll take them both."

"Okay," he rung up the items that Justin had, and Justin handed him the money. The cashier wrapped the items in a velvet box and handed them both to Justin.

"Thank you."

"I will," answered Justin as he walked out of the door to the bench that was just outside the makeup store.

While Justin was in the jewelry store, Meganlynn had been shopping for makeup. She had found some eyeliner that was sparkly and sliver. The mascara that she got was gold and glittering. Her eye shadow was going to be white shimmer with just a hint of glitter. She was in the checkout line when she looked and saw Justin sitting on the bench.

Justin watched the door eagerly and waited for her to come out. They still needed to buy shoes and accessories for her. Then, he saw someone else that he knew heading for the door as well.

"What are going in there for, Blue?"

"I'm getting makeup for my mother. She ran out of eyeliner." Then he turned to go into the store. Justin knew that he had to do something.

"Are you sure that it's not for yourself?" he spat out.

"I'm very sure," Blue said, turning back around and looking Justin right in the eyes.

"Really? I'm only asking because you look like you have a very thin line on your eyelids."

"Now, do I?"

"Yes." Justin looked in the window and saw that Meganlynn was still in the check-out line. "Or is that just a lame-line?"

"Or is that just a lame-line?" he mocked, turning toward Justin trying to pierce him with his eyes, which, since it was Blue, wasn't very scary.

"Now look, I have to go now. Meganlynn promised that she'd be at the store over there at eleven forty. I have to meet her there," he said, pointing at the jewelry store that he had just left.

"Oh, I'll go over there right now."

"No!"

"*No!* What?"

"Nothing."

"Afraid that I'm going to steal her away are we?"

"No."

"Maybe I should go and tell her for you, shouldn't I?"

"Sure, go ahead. That is if you can even get a word in before she calls security."

"I'll get a word in."

"Yeah right, believe whatever you want to believe."

"I'm going over there now."

"Go ahead, I want to see you come out, screaming like a little girl."

Blue screeched as he turned and walked into the jewelry store. At the same time, Meganlynn came out, and Justin pulled her toward their next destination: the shoe store.

"Hello there, sir," said the cashier to Blue. "How may I help you?" There still wasn't anybody in the store. Blue was startled to see that there wasn't anybody in there, especially Meganlynn. Blue thought long and hard for a minute and then had an idea pop into his mind; he was going to get Meganlynn something.

"I'm looking for something for some one that I like, but she doesn't have any idea that I like her, and she's absolutely obsessed with witchcraft."

"Want to say it with her favorite symbol then?"

"Yes, I would."

"Then come over here." The cashier pulled out a star with a circle around it. There were black diamonds that were placed in the circle, and it also had black-hills gold for the star with one of the blackest of black diamonds that Blue had ever seen in his life in the middle of it.

"What do you think of it?" the cashier asked.

"I love it and so will she."

"Good, that will be three hundred dollars."

"I can't do that. Can you settle for about thirty?"

"No, sorry, can't. I may be going out of business but I still need to take the sticker price for them, this is the final price."

"Whatever, thanks, but I better get going before she can get too far away from me."

⁓

Meganlynn and Justin were trying on shoes. They held the dress up to her when she had the different pairs of heels on. The dress was long on her anyway, so she had to get a very high pair of heels.

"I like these that I have on." She looked at the five-inch high heels' fake diamonds as they sparkled on her feet. The shoes had the crisscross just like the dress did. They were silver and had a golden cross where the crisscross was. The shoes didn't exactly cover her feet at all, and all of the shoes there had fake diamonds and sparkles all over them.

"Sure, so do I," Justin said back very rudely noticing that Blue was around and getting very upset about it.

"What is your problem?"

"Nothing! Nothing is my problem!" he shouted back at her.

"I'm just trying to be a good girlfriend and see if you're okay or not, that's all."

"You're so not a good girlfriend!" Justin was totally upset about the whole thing with Blue, and plus, he had just saw a couple of the guys that were passing by the shoe store checking her out as they walked by. In fact, a couple of the guys actually walked back and past her again just see her, and one person had actually come into the store to get a good look at her.

"How am I not a good girlfriend to you?"

"You only care about how many guys you meet, flirt with, and how many flirt back! Oh! And I almost forgot, your stupid writings! That's all that you care about!"

"No, it's not, and you know it," she said in a calming voice. Justin then realized what he had been doing when he saw a tear run down Meganlynn's face.

"Look, sweetheart, I'm sorry," he said, taking a step toward her as she took a step away from him.

"No," she whispered. *Just get away from me,* was what she was really thinking. She loved him deeply, but she also knew that this was going to happen sooner or later, so she had to end it right here and right now since he was yelling at her.

"What!" he screamed in her ear.

"I don't think that we should see each other anymore."

"Why not?"

"You just yelled at me; why shouldn't I want to end things here and now?"

"Because we're meant to be together."

"I know, Justin, we're meant to be together, but maybe not until later."

"But I want to marry you and have children with you."

"Yeah, well, me with you is never going to work out and you know it. You had to have known that this day was going to come and kill you one day. You just had to." A tear was running down her face and into her hands as she walked up to the cash register and paid for the shoes.

"What do I do now? Do you have your phone?"

"Yes, I do. Call your parents tell them that you were a jerk, I dumped your sorry butt on the ground, and also tell them that we are no longer having dinner with you guys tonight. You can come to the party but, thank goodness, we are allowed to sit next to whomever we wish on the way to band camp tomorrow. The ride should be fun wouldn't you say?" she asked sadly.

"Please, Megan, forgive me."

"For what?"

"I don't know, just forgive me."

"Learn what you did, make your heart right with God, and then maybe we'll talk."

"Fine! Be like that you dumb—blonde!"

"Yeah, that's a sure sign of intelligence, telling a girl that she's a dumb blonde when she just got her book published."

"Oh, you probably slept with the guys of the corporation for that publishing deal!"

Right at that moment, Meganlynn's parents walked around the corner to hear Justin screaming and Meganlynn crying. They also saw Meganlynn cry and try to turn away from him, but he wouldn't let her go even though she was telling him to.

"Get your hands off me! You're no better than Blue!" she shouted and then Justin released her immediately. She decided that she should just walk away from him and go with her parents.

"Come on, Justin, I'll take you home," Meganlynn's father told him.

"Fine," he said, walking out the door. Meganlynn looked up at her mother's face and her mother could see the tears in her eyes.

"Why don't you tell me about it over a pretzel, okay?"

"Yeah," cried Meganlynn. They then walked over to the pretzel stand and bought pretzels.

"What happened to you Meganlynn?"

"He just started to yell at me, and it scared me. Then he called me a dumb blonde. Then I said that sounds really intelligent by calling someone who just got their book published a dumb blonde, and then he said that I slept with all of the guys just to get my book published. I mean, with everything that I'm already going through, isn't that enough?" she asked, crying into her hands.

"You'd think wouldn't you?" her mother asked with one of her eyebrows getting higher than the other when she heard her daughter finally speak.

"I mean with everything that I'm already going through, isn't that enough?" Meganlynn asked, seeming to breath heavy and starting to cry.

"Yes." She wept and then lay her head down on the table.

"What do you mean *with everything that you're already going through, isn't that enough?*" her mother asked her. Her daughter looked up at her and pondered whether she should really tell her mother or not.

"Everything that's been going on between Blue and me for the past two days."

"What has been going on?" Her mother's voice got low.

"He started sexually harassing me again." Meganlynn then cried out and put her head back onto the table to cry.

"Then what did Justin say to you?" Her mother took a deep breath with her lips getting thinner and thinner.

"I think that Justin was mad. He was kind of acting like it. I can't stand to have him mad at me. And the worst part of it is that I don't really know what he's mad about."

"Wait, Justin was mad?"

"At me, and he never gets mad at me."

"Well, then, I think I know what he was pretty upset about."

"What?" Her mother pointed toward the one person that she didn't want to see, the one person that she didn't want to hear about, and definitely the last person that she even wanted to remotely think about.

"Blue," her mother said as she was pointing at him.

"What's he doing here?"

"I don't know, but I can tell you that Justin was probably just trying to cause a scene so he couldn't hurt you as bad or even at all."

"Oh," she said, starting to cry. She remembered every memory that they had had together and all that she had loved about him. She really wanted him back, to feel that touch that he had given her, and that she had experienced and loved about him. She needed Justin back with her.

"Are you going to see him soon?" her mother asked her.

"Tomorrow, and if he'll let me, I guess I can get him back then."

"Okay, Justin was really nice, and you didn't see the signs that he had given you."

"He didn't give me any signs, he just kind of drug me toward the shoe store, but I mean—I figured that was just because we had been short on time."

"Well, I guess we'd better get your dad on the phone and see what's going on with them."

"So, why did you say that she had slept with every guy in the company to get her book published?" Meganlynn's father asked Justin as they were driving out of the parking lot of the mall.

"I didn't know what to say," he started off. "It—"

"And you think that was the right thing to say?"

"No, but I mean—I mean—"

"Look, you were mad, I get it, but look don't go off calling my daughter a whore."

"Look, he was standing right behind her!"

"Who was standing right behind her?"

"Blue! He's been harassing her all week. Plus, I thought she was going to find someone else once she goes off on her publishing career, and Blue was stalking her, and I was just mad and scared all at the same time."

"Blue was behind her?"

"I caused a scene because he was right behind her, and I wanted to protect her."

"Thank you, I guess, but why didn't you come and get us? I mean we were only a phone call away." her father said once again. He couldn't believe that Blue would go to this much trouble just to get her attention. It was so stupid for him to do, and he was sure that Blue knew it.

"Yes, he was standing right behind her. I didn't want to scare her. I wanted to protect her and he had already followed us to her safe haven and I didn't want to make her feel more uncomfortable than she already had."

"Okay, how close was he to her?"

"About five feet away."

"So, he was standing right behind her, and then he was coming up closer and closer?"

"Sort of."

"If he wasn't doing that, then what was he doing?"

"He was just staring at her for no apparent reason, and it was making me feel really weird. He had that look as if he was going to take her and rape her. He really wants her sexually and nothing else. He was looking at her like no other girl that I've seen him look at. I mean, when he was looking at Holly Taylor, he never looked at her with the same intensity as he did with Meganlynn. And quite frankly, I miss her. I've never looked at her like that, sir."

"I know. You look at her with love and compassion."

"So, what are we going to do about today?"

"Well, I think that we can safely say that you were just trying to protect Meganlynn, but I still don't know if she wants to talk to you or not."

"I know, making a scene was probably a really stupid thing for me to do."

"Well, yeah it was probably one of the stupidest things that you could do but it kept Blue away from her."

"Really, how?"

"You were trying to protect her from something that you knew was going to harm her. I appreciate that very much," he said then, turning the car back around.

"Where are we going?" Justin asked again.

"We are going back to the mall we just left."

"Why?"

"Well, I think that Meganlynn deserves to hear the truth from you and not from anyone else."

Finally, they returned back to the mall. Justin and Meganlynn's father went and found Meganlynn and her mother sitting at the pretzel shop. Meganlynn then fell into Justin's arms and hugged him as soon as she saw him.

A little tear was running down her face, and she knew that she was able to forgive him for yelling at her and not telling her what was going on.

"I love you," Justin whispered in her ear.

"Love you, too," she whispered back in his ear.

"Did you call your parents yet?" she asked while she was taking a step back and then looked into his eyes with her eyes while trying to wipe the tears from her eyes.

"No," I figured that I would tell them once I got home." They both smiled at one another and then hugged once again. They were happy to be in one another's arms once again, even if they were just going to be in the mall for a short while longer.

Justin's eyes then got huge as Meganlynn got a tap on the shoulder from Blue. Meganlynn turned around and looked to see Blue standing right behind her. She took a step back to make sure that she was in Justin's arms.

"What do you want?" Justin asked very sternly.

"Just wanted to come over and see if everything was okay between you two. I would hate for you two to break up and for my chance to happen," Blue answered back sarcastically.

"Yeah, because that would actually happen," her father whispered under his breath.

"It would," Blue shot back, keeping his eyes on Meganlynn. Meganlynn just kept her mouth shut and kept her eyes on the floor. "Wouldn't it Meganlynn?" he asked, reaching out to grab her shirt. She pulled away and tried to go more into Justin's arms. She brought her eyes up to his level to make sure that he wasn't going to try anything else.

"Don't touch my daughter," her father said.

"Do you think I care what you say?"

"Obviously not," her mother walked away as she was starting to get fed-up with all of this.

Her mother showed up a few seconds later with mall security.

Meganlynn told them everything that had happened between them.

"We'll just have to see and we'll have to have this checked out. But the best thing that we can do is give you the local police's number and if you see him anywhere around you again then give them a call and tell them what's been going on. We are only mall security not real cops, sorry miss," he handed Meganlynn a card with the phone number on it.

"Thank you," her father and mother both said, and Meganlynn nodded her head.

After the mall security had left, Meganlynn's father looked down at the box that was in her hands.

"What's that?" he asked her.

"A present from Blue that is so horrible that it doesn't even deserve to be out of the box."

"Can I see it?" he asked her, holding out his hand.

"Sure," she then gave the box to her father and was happy to get rid of it.

"What is it?"

"It's the sign of a devil worshipper. Hold it up to the light, you'll see why it's so horrible."

"Okay," he held it up to the light and read the reading that was in the star. Her father was quiet, and they knew what was going through his mind: *I'm going to kill him for doing all of this to my daughter.*

"Are you okay, honey?" her mother finally asked.

"After we go and eat dinner with Justin's parents we are going to go and fill out a police report against this boy. He's harassing poor Meganlynn so much, it's not even funny. I want to personally kill him, but that's just because you could see the look on his face. The one that he was giving Meganlynn was horrible," her father answered back looking in the review mirror at his daughter. Then Meganlynn's phone started to ring.

"Hello?" she answered.

"If you go to the police," the voice started. She recognized the voice immediately and knew what she had to do. She immediately put it on speaker phone. "If you even think of going to the police, for that matter, you can kiss your sorry little life good-bye because I will kill you and they will never find the body. They will all think you either ran away because of me, or you are being hidden by me from the police. They will never find you, not in a million years, because the only people that you are going to be meeting are the people in hell. I will have you personally thrown into hell for everything that you have done to me. Hear me?"

"Yes, I hear you, and to let you know, the only people that I will be seeing are the people that you aren't. If you kill me, at least I won't have to be on earth with you and the rest of the scumbags like you. I will be in heaven with my dead relatives, but the dead are not really dead because they are not dead in Christ. They are alive in Christ, which is very much what I am. I will not be hell, but I will be in heaven with God. If you are Satan and have me thrown into hell personally, I don't think that'll last very long."

"You are so not a Christian!"

"How am I not a Christian?"

"You dress too slutty to be a Christian, and you act like a hooker during school. We need you so us guys can get our jollies on through you."

"I haven't given anything like that to anyone."

"Good, then I'll be the one to take it away."

"No, you're not. I think I'll wait for my husband."

"No, I'm the one that's going to take your virginity."

"No, you're not."

"Then I'll make me your guy."

"Good luck with that," she said. She couldn't hang up the phone. Her father was finally back at the little circle with the mall security guard. He then listened in with the tape recorder that he had on him for the day.

"Meganlynn, I will get your virginity if it's the last thing I do!"

"What did you say that you're going to do if I go and tell the police again?"

"Kill you! How can such a dumb blonde forget something like that?"

"You said it, I'm a dumb blonde."

"Good point."

"So you're probably still with that moron Justin. What do you like about him?"

"Okay, Meganlynn give the phone over to the security guard and let him handle it."

"Happily," she said as she handed the phone over.

"Blue, sir, this is mall security, and I would just like you to know that we have been taping this message, and we will use this in court against you. See you in court; they will charge you as an adult for everything you have done." Then he hung up the phone. He then handed it back to Meganlynn to take with her. She took a deep breath and then went on with the rest of the day.

CHAPTER 4

The plane ride was compelling for Meganlynn. She still had Justin, but he was not going to be able to stop Blue from harassing her; he was only going to be able to stop him for a little while. Knowing Blue, the second that he was standing, Blue would be right back in the spot that Justin was sitting in and there would be a huge fight, and then they would both be sent home.

"Hey guys," said Lizzie when they got to the airport. Meganlynn's parents walked them in and said their good-byes at the gate. The plane had another hour and a half before it took off. Mr. Nolls wanted them there an hour and a half early to check-in and let them have a good time with their friends before leaving for a week in Arizona.

Meganlynn was okay as long as they were on the ground, but once they were on the plane and then off into the air, things went all wrong for her.

"I have to go to the bathroom, Meganlynn. Do you mind if I go?" asked Justin.

"Why are you asking me? If you have to go, then go."

"Okay, I'll be right back." He got up and left the front part of the plane. Immediately after Justin was not visible anymore, Blue got into the seat that Justin had been sitting in.

"What are you up to, cutie?"

"My name isn't cutie, and go away, I'm really starting to hate you."

"Naw, I think I'll stay right here," he said, putting his hand right on her legs so she could feel them.

"Get your hands off me!" she shouted moving the rest of the way so she could get away from him.

"No. You see, you're such a slut that you'll do anything that I want to do, won't you?"

"No. Now, get your hands off me and let me be. I just want to finish reading my book."

"What's your book called?"

"*Revelation: The Scroll and the Lamb.*"

"Sounds interesting. What's it about?"

"It's about everything that is going to be going on in the end times."

"When are the end times going to happen?"

"No one but God knows."

"Yeah right, you slut!" he shouted, slapping her across the face. She was in dire pain and needed some help with the gash he had just put on her face. She put her hand up to her face. When she brought it back down, she saw that there was blood coming off of her hands.

"I'm not a slut!"

"How do you know that?"

"Because I've done nothing that a slut does."

"How would you come to that conclusion?"

"Pretty much because I'm a Christian, and I witness to people instead of having sex with them. A slut is someone who has sex with every guy that she meets, and a normal person is someone that follows the world, but a Christian is someone that never, ever gives up trying to preach His word and obeys His laws like not having sex before you are married."

"You're still not a Christian."

"How?"

"Because you don't know the Bible word for word."

"You can know the Bible word for word and still not be a Christian."

"Fine then tell me one thing that I am going to experience that you aren't."

"Total and complete hell," she answered back under her breath.

"Really, and if your God comes back right now, what I am I going to go through here on earth that you won't?"

"You're just letting me have even more fun right here, you know that?"

"How?"

"I get to preach your ear off," she said as she looked up Revelation in her Bible.

"Found it yet?"

"Yup," she answered. "Here it is: Revelation 6: 1-17. It says right here: This is after the rapture and this is everything that is going to be going on during the Seven Years of Tribulation.

"I watched as the Lamb opened the first of the seven seals. Then I heard one of the four living creatures say in a voice like thunder, 'Come!' I looked, and there before me was a white horse! Its rider held a bow, and he was given a crown, and he rode out as a conqueror bent on conquest.

"When the Lamb opened the second seal, I heard the second living creature say, 'Come!' Then another horse came out, a fiery red one. Its rider was given the power to take peace from the earth and make men slay each other. To him was given a large sword.

"When the Lamb opened the third seal, I heard the third living creature say, 'Come!' I looked, and there before me was a black horse! It rider was holding a pair of scales in his hand. Then I heard what sounded like a voice among the four living creatures, saying, 'A quart of wheat for a day's wages, and three quarts of barley for a day's wage, and do not damage the oil and wine!'

"When the Lamb opened the fourth seal, I heard the voice of the fourth living creature say, 'Come!' I looked, and there before me was a pale horse! Its rider was named Death and Hades was following close behind him. They were given power over a fourth of the earth to kill by sword, famine, and plague, and by the wild beasts of the earth.

"When he opened the fifth seal, I saw under the alter the souls of those who had been slain because of the word of God and the testimony they had maintained. They called out in a loud voice, 'How long, Sovereign Lord, holy and true, until you judge the inhabitants of the earth and avenge our blood?' Then each of them was given a white robe, and they were told to wait a little longer, until the number of their fellow servants and brothers who were to be killed as they had been was completed.

"I watched as he opened the sixth seal. There was a great earthquake. The sun turned black like sackcloth made of goat hair, the whole moon turned blood red, and the stars in the sky fell to earth, as late figs drop from a fig tree when shaken by a strong wind. The sky receded like a scroll, rolling up, and every mountain and island was removed from its place.

"Then the kings of the earth, the princes, the generals, the rich, the mighty, and every slave and every free man hid in caves and among the rocks of the mountains. They called to the mountains and rocks, 'Fall on us and hide us from the face of him who sits on the throne and from the wrath of the Lamb! For the great day of their wrath has come, and who can stand?'"

"Wow, what was that supposed to mean?" asked Blue when she was done with her speech.

"Oh, Blue, I'm not even done!" She then flipped through her Bible more until she came to Revelation 8:6-21.

"Where are you going now?"

"Right here: Revelation 8:6-21, The Trumpets.

"Then, the seven angels who had the seven trumpets prepared to sound them.

"The first angel sounded his trumpet, and there came hail and fire mixed with blood, and it was hurled down upon the earth. A third of the earth was burned up, and a third of the trees were burned up, and all of the green grass was burned up.

"The second angel sounded his trumpet, and something like a huge mountain, all ablaze, was thrown into the sea. A third of the sea turned to blood, a third of the living creatures in the sea died, and a third of the ships were destroyed.

"The third angel sounded his trumpet, and a great star, blazing like a torch, fell from the sky on a third of the rivers and on the springs of water—the name of the star is Wormwood. A third of the waters turned bitter, and many people died from the waters that became bitter.

"The fourth angel sounded his trumpet, and a third of sun was struck, a third of the moon, a third of the stars, so that a third of them turned dark. A third of the day was without light, and also a third of the night.

"As I watched, I heard an eagle that was flying in mid-air called out in a loud voice: 'Whoa! Whoa! Woe to the inhabitants of the earth, because of the trumpet blasts about to be sounded by the other three angels!'

"The fifth angel sounded his trumpet, and I saw a star that had fallen from the sky to the earth. The star was given the key to the shaft of the Abyss. When he opened the Abyss, smoke rose from it like the smoke of a gigantic furnace. The sun and sky were darkened by the smoke from the Abyss. And out of the smoke locusts came down upon the earth and were given power like that of scorpions of the earth. They were told not to harm the grass of the earth or any plant or tree, but only to torture those people who did not have the seal of God on their foreheads. They were not given the power to kill them, but only to torture them for five months. And the agony they suffered was like that of the sting of a scorpion when it strikes a man. During those days men will seek death, but will not find it; they will long to die, but death will elude them.

"The locusts looked like horses prepared for battle. On their heads they wore something like crowns of gold, and their faces resembled human faces. Their hair was like a woman's hair, and their teeth were like a lion's teeth. They had breastplates of iron, and the sound of their wings was like the thundering of many horses and chariots rushing into battle. They had tails and stings like scorpions, and in their tails had the power to torture people for five months. They had as king over them the angel of Abyss, whose name in Hebrew is Abaddon, and in Greek, Apollyon.

"The first woe is past; two other woes are yet to come.

"The sixth angel sounded his trumpet, and I heard a voice coming from the horns of the golden alter that is before God. It said to the sixth angel who had the trumpet, 'Release the four angels who are bound at the great river Euphrates.' And the four angels who had kept ready for this very hour and day and month and year were released to kill a third of mankind.

"The horses and riders I saw in my vision looked like this: Their breastplates were fiery red, dark blue, and yellow as sulfur. The heads of the horses resembled the heads of lions, and out of their mouths came fire, smoke and sulfur. A third of mankind was killed by these three plagues of fire, smoke and sulfur that came out of their mouths. The power of the horses was in their mouths and in their tails; for their tails were like snakes, heaving heads with which they inflict injury.

"The rest of mankind that were not killed by these plagues still did not repent of the work of their hands; they did not stop worshiping demons, and idols of gold, silver, bronze, stone and wood—idols that cannot see or hear or walk. Nor did they repent of their murders, their magic arts, their sexual immorality or their thefts."

Blue had had his arm around her the whole time she was speaking and had his other arm on her leg. He had just used the Bible toward his own personal gain, but Meganlynn knew what to do. Justin had walked up right behind her when she had started preaching to Blue, but kept silent because he wanted him to hear the word of the Lord for once in his life.

"Now what was the whole point in that?" he asked as he moved his hand farther and farther up her leg. Meganlynn was finally sick of it and decided that enough was enough.

"That was so you can get ready for what's coming when the rapture happens, and I won't be here!" she shouted in his face. It made him jump back a little bit, but he was still sitting right next to her.

"Now, why would I care?"

"Because of this," she held up the Bible and shoved it in his face. "Now, get out of Justin's seat and stay away from me!" He took her Bible out of her hands when he got up to leave.

"This means nothing!"

"To you! It means everything to me!"

"Fine! Then keep it!" he threw it back in her face so most of the pages of the Bible flew out and onto the ground.

"You'll answer for that, one day!"

Then he went and sat back down in his own seat while Meganlynn and Justin picked up the pages to the Bible that had fallen out.

"Are you going to call your parents about this?" Justin asked, getting some of the pages back into the Bible.

"Guess I better," Meganlynn answered. "But I'll wait until we land and then I'll make the phone call."

"Okay, just make sure that you get a new one," he said holding up the Bible that had all of the pages all scattered and some still falling out.

"I will," she answered, taking the Bible from his hands. "Poor thing," she said, trying to straighten all of the pages back into the original binding. Meganlynn smiled a little. Justin smiled back at her at the most that he could. He wrapped his arm around her and walked her back to her seat.

"Don't want to be here, do you?" Justin asked when he decided that she had been staring out the window for too long of a time.

"Not at all, Justin, not at all," she answered, thinking about when times were easier between the two of them and Blue was nowhere near the picture to be found.

"Where would you rather be?"

"At home, safe and sound from all harm."

"Okay, I guess I can see that."

"You guess?" she repeated with a joking voice.

"Yeah, I guess."

"How can you guess?"

"I don't know, I just can."

"You don't even realize everything that I'm going through, do you?" Her voice had disgust in it when she said these words to him.

"Meg—"

"No, you listen. You try being sexually harassed and then forced to sit next to the same person that did it to you in the first place. You try being sexually harassed, harassed, then stalked, and then you tell me how you feel and whether you'd rather be at home where no one can bother you what so ever."

"I see your point."

"Good." Then she began to cry.

"Meg, what's wrong?"

"Do you have a notebook?"

"No."

"Never mind, there's one in here."

"What are you going to do with that?"

"Write like I love to do."

"Okay." Then for the rest of the plane ride she wrote. The first thing that she wrote was a poem that explained the different things that she was going through. She didn't exactly feel like writing a short story or a novel, so she copied down Bible verses.

One of the verses that she wrote down was Lamentations 1:16:

> This is why I weep
> And my eyes over flow with tears.
> No one is near to comfort me,
> No one to restore my spirit.
> My children are destitute
> Because the enemy has prevailed.

She wrote down many things from Lamentations and from Revelations as well as Romans. She didn't have quite enough time to copy down all her favorite Bible verses, but she had enough time to copy down the verses that explained how she was feeling at the moment.

Finally, the plane ride ended, and she and Justin got off. Then, Mr. Nolls told them that they were to be back by ten o'clock that evening. Justin and Meganlynn took off to find the rental car that her parents had gotten for her.

CHAPTER 5

Meganlynn loved Arizona and already knew that she did from the trip that she and her parents had taken when she was in fifth grade. Once she was finally in the rental vehicle for the first time, she pulled out a CD from her purse. It was her favorite band, Spoon. They were Christian rock, and she had all of their CDs.

They listened to that while Meganlynn drove to the gas station where she called her parents.

"Hey," she said once her mother finally answered.

"Hi, honey, what's up? Are you on the ground?"

"Yeah, and I need those addresses."

"Okay, do you have a pen and pencil handy?"

"Yeah."

"Who are you going to go and see first?"

"Probably Uncle Bob and Aunt Cindy."

"Okay, well they live on Wells Road.

"Okay, thanks. Now what about the Gollingbird address?"

"They live right next to Aunt Cindy and Uncle Bob."

"Thank you."

"Yeah, and we put that money in your account."

"Thanks."

"Yeah, and the weird part of it was that Grandma and Aunt Cherie wanted to put two hundred dollars apiece in so spend wisely and bring them back some gifts for the family."

"Okay, we get the whole last day for shopping anyway."

"Okay, I'll see you next week."

Once they were finally there, her Aunt Cindy and Uncle Bob were very surprised to see her.

"Who's this?" she asked, pointing to Justin.

"This is Justin, my boyfriend."

"Oh," she said, looking at him. "Well come on in, come in."

"Thank you," she answered.

"Would you kids like something to drink?"

"Please," answered Meganlynn.

"What are you two down here for?"

"Band camp."

"Then what are you doing out here?"

"Well, we're allowed out during the night time, and we just got here. My parents rented me a car so now I'm here."

"Can you show me where the bathroom is?" asked Justin.

"Sure can," Uncle Bob said and then took Justin to the bathroom.

"You do realize that the Johnny guy next door can never stop talking about you, right?"

"Really?" Meganlynn asked excitedly. "And wait, Johnny lives next door to you?"

"Yeah, I can get your Uncle Bob to distract that Justin kid and you can go over and flirt a little if you want to."

"But I'm only going to go over and say 'hi.'"

"I think that it would be better if I stayed over here or got Justin to go with me when and if I do go over there," Meganlynn replied.

"Okay, I'll tell Uncle Bob."

"Tell Uncle Bob what? I don't want to go over there by myself. I actually love this guy, he's stuck with me through everything and I can't imagine leaving him for another guy."

"But, he said that if you ever came down to visit then we had to send you over by yourself, or if we got a picture then we had to give him a copy," her aunt's face begged her to go and see him.

"And I will go and see him once Justin comes back from the bathroom and I can take him with me."

"But that's no fun."

"Maybe not for you but I'm in love with Justin. I love him so much it's not even funny," a real smile broke on her face for the first time in a long time.

"Fine, but promise that you'll go," her aunt said getting puppy-dog eyes.

"Fine," she said as Justin and her uncle came back into the room.

"Go where?" Justin asked walking over to Meganlynn.

"Going over to Johnny's house," she answered him.

"Who's Johnny?"

"A boy from my past," Meganlynn answered irritably.

"Okay," Justin answered making sure not to pry too much in front of her aunt and uncle.

"We better get going," Meganlynn said.

"Fine," her aunt answered, showing them to the door. "But make sure that you go and see them," she demanded after they finally got out of the door.

"We will," Meganlynn answered while her aunt slammed the door in her face. "Bye," she finished.

"Do you want to go and see your past?" he asked.

"No, he moved the summer before I really got to know you."

"Then that was years ago, why does he want you to go and see him?"

"He liked me."

"Oh, does he still?"

"Don't know," she took a deep breath. "But someone's watching in the window," she motioned in back of her. "So we better keep a promise or I will have more problems than Blue in my family," she said, taking his hand and starting to walk toward to the house across the street. When they got there, she took a deep breath and knocked on the door.

"Why don't you want to be here?" Justin asked.

"I don't want to remember my past. It'll only make me want it more," Meganlynn replied.

"Hey," Johnny's mother answered the door with the sound of surprise in her voice.

"Hey, Mrs. Gollingbird," Meganlynn said.

"Meganlynn?"

"Yeah, and this is Justin, my boyfriend."

"Oh, well then, come in. Come in! Johnny will be so pleased that you're here. He never can stop talking about you."

"It should be nice to see him again," she answered taking Justin's hand.

"He's been waiting for a chance to see you since well, for forever as he puts it. Every vacation we take is always, 'Can we go north and see Meganlynn?' After a while though, it did get a little old," she chuckled.

"Yes, I know."

"How is everything?" she asked, climbing up the stairs to go to Johnny's room.

"Pretty good."

"Good. I'll go and get Johnny, I'll be right back."

Finally, he came downstairs.

Johnny's dark brown hair was curly and came down to his ears. He had on the blue and white sweatshirt that Meganlynn had given him five years earlier. He had a pair of blue jeans on also and white socks. His deep blue eyes won out in the battle of the eyes. She never had a crush on anyone like she had a crush on Johnny. She had wanted everything to be perfect.

"Meganlynn?" he asked. Maybe that daydream wasn't just a daydream at all. Maybe God had sent her a vision to be careful.

"Johnny."

"What are you doing here?" he asked. The vision was out of line.

"My school is having band camp down here."

"That's great! Where at?"

"The university."

"Oh, so then who's this? I don't remember seeing him up there."

"This is Justin. He's my wonderful

"But, you were supposed to be sin

under his breath.

"Sorry that I'm not," Meganlynn answ

"Well," Johnny said, suddenly making it

the two of them standing there.

"So I take it that you're Johnny?" Justin asked.

"Yeah," Johnny answered bluntly.

"Why didn't you wait for me?" Johnny asked.

"Wait for what? For you to come back north? I don't know. Maybe it was that I fell in love," Meganlynn answered back.

"Fell in love? Oh please, you can't even begin to spell love."

"I'm sorry, Johnny, but I never thought that we would see each other again."

"Fine," he answered still disappointed.

"We better get going," Meganlynn said standing up.

"Fine, but can I at least get your number?"

"Sure," she answered getting out her phone. He programmed her number into his phone and she the same. Justin stood there with his arm around Meganlynn's waist.

"Bye," he said, hugging her good bye. After Meganlynn had left and was already half way to her aunt and uncle's house, she looked back and saw Johnny looking out the window at her. She smiled at him and let out a little chuckle. She gave him a little wave and then went back into her aunt and uncle's house.

CHAPTER 6

Nothing about the morning was cold or hot. The weather was perfect for the day of band camp that was ahead of them. They ate breakfast and then went out onto the field.

Mr. Nolls had them set up where they were going to in the first place. Unfortunately, Blue was always right behind Meganlynn for the whole thing. Then Mr. Nolls had to do something with a different part of the group and wasn't paying attention to Meganlynn's section.

"Roses are red, violets are blue. Who really loves and wants you? How far will they go to get it?" Blue asked Meganlynn as they sat down on the grass.

"Shut-up, Blue."

"Why should I?" he asked, rubbing her back. Unfortunately, Justin was on the other side of the field.

"Stop, please," she begged. Tears were already starting to run down her face.

"What is your issue with me?"

"You're sexually harassing me."

"Deal with it," he slapped her across the face softly. "Hon, you have to learn to deal with it. Life is filled with people like me, and you will just have to learn that life is never fair either. This is why you belong with me."

"Don't call me 'hon' I'm not your honey. I'm not even yours."

"How do you know this?" He looked deep into her eyes, and then she had nothing to say anymore. She needed a comeback that was as good as the punch he had just thrown at her from behind.

"Because—"

"Because you've been asking for it to happen."

"I never asked for it to happen." She had her doubts about it not being her fault.

"Yes you did." He was sure that he was right.

"How did I ask for it?"

"Your body," he said, running his hands up and down her sides for a minute. "Your figure." His face then touched her neck.

"Get off me!"

"You're telling me to get off of you when you're all on me?"

"Stop!"

"No."

"Just let me go," she cried.

"Break!" Mr. Nolls shouted out of the blue.

"Thank you, Lord," Meganlynn said under her breath. Justin did not even rush over; he really just let her friends handle it.

"What happened?" one of her friends, Britney, asked.

"Nothing," she answered, looking for Blue and Justin. Finally, she found Blue and she found Justin. They were talking together, freely. They were laughing together.

"Britney," Meganlynn started out. "Why are Blue and Justin both talking to each other?"

"Maybe they're in a fight."

"When they're laughing?"

"Good point."

"Wow, what a dirt bag."

"Give me one minute."

"To do what?"

"You'll see," she answered walking over to where Blue and Justin were both standing.

"You jerk!" Brittany shouted in his face.

"For what?" Justin asked Britney as she was shouting in his face.

"Hmmm…let's see—you're chatting with your girl-friend's sexual harasser! Wow you really are a jerk!" Then she walked back to Meganlynn. Meganlynn cried a little harder than she was already.

"Meganlynn, what was that about?" Justin came back over and shouted in her face.

"I don't know! You honestly think that I had some-thing to do with that?" she shouted back.

"Yeah! She's one of your friends!"

"Doesn't mean that she doesn't have a mind of her own!"

"Fine, you want to play that game?" He was close to her face. She knew what was going to happen next.

"You don't care about anyone but yourself!"

"Meganlynn!" shouted Britney.

"Don't worry about it," Meganlynn told her. She just took it as Justin was giving it to her.

"We're done," Meganlynn's voice cracked, letting him know that she didn't want to but felt as if she had to out of fear.

"Okay! I really never liked you in the first place! What am I saying? I really liked you, but after you did this, I don't care anymore, and I do too care about other people!"

"No you don't!"

"Bye!" Then she walked away. She didn't cry out of sadness but more out of fear. She missed him already, but she knew that it had to end at some point.

Finally, it was time to go back out on the field. The band was trying to get from one place to the other, and they eventually made it. Then it was lunch time.

"What is this?" asked Blue as he grabbed Meganlynn's butt.

"That is my butt!" screamed Meganlynn as she turned around to face him, taking her butt away from him. "Keep your hands off it!" Then she walked away. She was trying to keep to herself together without crying even harder.

"Well, don't know if I can quite do that." He was trying to sound sexy.

"Then try your hardest not to!"

"Okay, but I just want to tell you something."

"What?"

"You'll never be out of my sight."

All lunch, he grabbed her sides and then tried to touch her where he would never be allowed. Meganlynn wanted to punch him if he touched her one more time.

She found a little hole in the ground and took her Bible out and read it. She had fifteen minutes to read it, and hopefully no one would ever find her right there. She decided to read a little bit more of Jeremiah.

"Jeremiah 33:11: Give thanks to the Lord Almighty, for the Lord is good; his love endures forever," she repeated this five times to herself to remember for all the time that she was at band camp. Then she read more out loud to herself to comfort herself more and more through these hard times.

"Revelation 11:15, The Seventh Trumpet: The seventh angel sounded his trumpet, and there were loud voices in heaven, which said: The kingdom of the world has become the kingdom of our Lord and of his Christ, and he will reign forever and ever. The Harvest of the Earth, Revelation 14: I looked and there before me was a white cloud, and seated on the cloud was one 'like the son of man' with a crown of gold on his head and a sharp sickle in his hand. Then another angel came out of the temple and called in a loud voice to him who was sitting on the cloud, 'Take your sickle and reap, because the time to reap has come and the harvest of the earth is ripe.' So he who was on the cloud swung his sickle over the earth and the earth was harvested. Revelation 15, Seven Angels With Seven Plagues: I saw in heaven another great and marvelous sign: seven angels with the seven last plagues—last, because with them God's wrath is completed. And I saw what looked like a sea of glass mixed with fire and, standing beside the sea, those who had been victorious over the beast and his image and over the number of his name."

She needed the comfort from God, but she could not feel it anywhere she went. She knew that none of the stuff that was going on was God's fault. She was panicking, and she knew it. She walked back into the cafeteria to find her friends that were normally right there by her side during everything.

"Meganlynn," said Britney, pulling her over to where Justin and Blue were standing. Britney stood in between Meganlynn and Blue, but Meganlynn and Justin were standing right across from each other.

"Yes?" Meganlynn asked Justin.

"Why did you get mad at me like that?" he asked, giving her his puppy-dog look.

"I don't know, Justin. Maybe because I am going through such an emotional time that I just may be so crazy I go all wrong all of the sudden like I did."

"Really?"

"No, I have a brain."

"Then, why did Britney come over and start yelling at me?"

"That was her own decision, not mine."

"Yeah, right! You had a part in it!"

"No, I didn't, I had nothing to do with that."

"Justin," started Britney, putting her hand on his back. "She really didn't have anything to do with me yelling at you."

"Oh, well, why didn't you tell me that before?"

"You wouldn't let me, and whenever she would try to tell you, you wouldn't listen to her."

"Okay, sorry." He rolled his eyes.

"I'm not the one that you should be apologizing to," Brittany snapped back.

"Why not? I didn't believe you."

"No, you didn't believe Meganlynn over there. You believed me."

"So what's so wrong with what I'm saying? Am I that much of a liar? Have I ever actually told you a lie about me or what I have done in the past?" asked Meganlynn with her eyes huge and her voice crackling. A tear ran down her cheek.

"There's nothing wrong with what you are saying. You aren't that much of a liar; I was just being a jerk because I thought that you were trying to break us up. No, you have actually never told me a lie about you or what you have done in the past."

"Look, Meganlynn, I am so sorry," Justin pleaded with her with his hands in a prayer position. He tried to hug her, but she could not handle it and pulled away.

"What are you sorry for?" Her eyes were now big, and you could see the deep blue that was in them. The pain, sadness, and hurt was also all shown in her eyes as she looked at him, asking him this question.

"Honestly, Meganlynn, I have absolutely no idea what you are so mad at me for!" He was shouting at her again.

"Then you can watch me walk away." She turned to walk away, crying again.

"No, don't walk away from me." He grabbed her arm. "Can I have a few seconds with you?"

"Sure." She walked forward a little to walk away.

"Meganlynn?" Britney asked Meganlynn.

"I can go on alone," Meganlynn assured her.

"Okay." Then Britney watched as Meganlynn, Blue, and Justin all went over to the corner of the hallway.

"What?" Meganlynn spat out when they were finally around the corner to where no one else could see.

"Why are you so mad at me?"

"If you can't figure it out, then maybe you don't need to know."

"Yes, I do need to know, Meganlynn. I need to know because I want to know why you are so mad at me."

"You want to know what I am so mad at you about, then you need to take a look at who and what you just started hanging around recently."

"Blue?"

"Yeah, there, now you know what's been bugging me the whole live-long day." Then she turned to walk away. She was about two steps away from the corner when she felt a hand on her shoulder trying to make her stay back with them.

"Blue," she started removing his hand from her shoulder, and turning to face him. "Get your hands off of me."

"Why should I?"

"Just because you are harassing me, doesn't mean that you can treat me however you freaking want to."

"Yes, it does."

"No, it doesn't."

"Yes it does." Then Blue struck her again. She sat on the ground in pain as the stinging in her face would not go away from where he had struck her this time. There was probably going to be a large bruise across her face from where his hand hit her face.

Meganlynn walked right back around to where they had taken her before and then looked at the two of them with her bruised face. She hoped that Justin and Blue both felt at least a little bit of remorse for what they had done to her. She hoped that they knew what they had done. She hoped that Blue got the point that the police could finally arrest him now for assault and for battery.

"Look," Blue started as she walked by. He said this just loud enough so she could hear it. "She thinks, she's going to go tell." He said it kind of a sweet and innocent voice like he had done nothing to her. "You poor, poor thing."

"Stay away from me." She then walked away from them. Blue was not very happy with her anyway.

"You tell any one of your little brainless friends, and they will never ever find you again because you will experience the beating of your life to where it is so hard that even your grandchildren would have a bruise—if you were to have any that is, and the only way that you are getting pregnant from now on is from me." He leaned forward to kiss her, but she pulled away just in time for him to miss.

She hated him, even more than ever before. She had not hated any one before in her life besides him. He had made her so mad, self-conscious, and scared all because he was a self-centered little spirit. "No, Meganlynn, we are going to do this right this time."

"No, please." Then he kissed her. It was the most disgusting thing in her life. The look on her face told all of it; he was all about himself, and she had not wanted that kiss to happen at all. He had just made it happen all on his own.

"You can go now, honey."

"I'm not your honey," she said as she ripped away from him and ran back to her cabin. She lay on her bed and cried for a minute. Then she whipped out her little journal that had everything that he had been doing and wrote the rest of the things that he had done to her that day. Then she got into her bag and pulled out a sweatshirt.

One of the girls who was in her cabin walked in to see her crying and noticed the journal lying wide-open on her bed. The girl picked up the journal and then looked at her.

"Has he really been doing all of this stuff to you?" she asked.

"Yes, he has," she cried out. Hardly any of her words were able to be made out, but her friend did her best to.

"You need to tell someone about this."

"I know. I know."

"Then why don't you? You're not stupid. Trust me, I know you're not stupid."

"I know, but he keeps on threatening me if I do tell someone. He just threatened me about the scar that's across my face at the moment."

"What did he say?"

"He said that if I told someone then I was never going to be found, because the beating that he was going to give me was going to be so harsh that my grandchildren were going to have bruises on them from the beating. Then he said that I would never have grandchildren because I would never do anything like that with anyone except for him, and then he forced me to kiss him."

"Where was your boyfriend all this time?"

"Justin's not my boyfriend anymore."

"Well he should still stick up for you."

"You'd think wouldn't you?"

"Yeah, where was he?"

"He was standing right there, watching as he did this to me."

"Well, come on, we need to get back down to band camp. I won't tell anyone, but if I find that he has done something else to you again, you will be telling someone because there won't be any other choice with me around."

"Okay." Meganlynn sniffled, and then they walked down to the field once again. The journal was still open on her bed, but Meganlynn really didn't care who read it; she wanted someone else to read it. She wanted enough people to read it that they could get a group together to find Blue and treat him the same way that he had been treating her since the first day of pre-camp.

Blue was the same; he had treated her the same way as he did when it was morning. He had pulled her onto his lap once again, and once again, no one told him to stop. Alex saw, but since he wasn't hitting her, Meganlynn told her to just back off. Her friends were furious that she was now just going along with it and then just writing everything down in her journal to get everything out because they all knew that writing alone wasn't going to be enough for Meganlynn. After the five hours of butt grabbing, lap pulling, and everything else that Blue was doing to her was over, the first day of band camp was finally over. Meganlynn pulled her sweatshirt around her as far as it would go and took everything that she had back up to her cabin. Meganlynn intended to take full advantage of it.

Her phone started to ring. She recognized the number as Johnny's and answered it.

"Hello?" she asked, her voice sounding tired and cracking.

"Hey, Meganlynn," answered Johnny's bright and cheery voice. "Are you free from band now?"

"Yeah, until ten that is."

"Okay, do you want to go out while you're still here?"

"You mean like on a date?"

"Yeah, on a date. It would be a double date, but yeah, on a date."

"Okay, what should I wear?"

"Heels, and then whatever you want. Your mom told me that you liked heels."

"Okay," she answered, looking for a pair of heels. "And I do love heels, by the way."

"Got anything that you want to wear but you never get to?"

"Yeah, but I think I left it at home. Don't worry, I'll look amazing."

"Okay, well, get ready, and I'll be over there in a half hour or so."

"Okay, I'll see you then."

"Who was that?" asked Lizzie.

"That was someone who wants to take me out on a date."

"Okay. You want some help?"

"I only have a half hour before they get here."

"We can make this work."

"Okay. He said that he didn't care what I wear, but I have to wear high heels."

"Okay. We can really make this work then."

"Really?"

Then the preparation started. Lizzie had the time of her life dressing up Meganlynn in her high-heeled boots and t-shirt. She had her all pretty for her date, and she also had everything ready for her to take with her.

"Meganlynn, who was scared to walk out onto the field, I present to you fearless Meganlynn. The way that you have been treated today makes you eligible for a younight. Now, don't let Justin or Blue or anyone else ruin this night for you."

"Okay." She left to walk out and find Johnny and his car. Johnny was driving a pale blue mustang convertible. She knew that she would only be with him for a few hours, but all in all, he was her guardian for tonight.

"Wow, Meganlynn, you look amazing."

"Thank you."

"Well, climb in to the passenger seat, and then we can go."

"Meganlynn wait!" yelled a voice and Meganlynn turned around to see Justin and Blue standing right behind her.

"What?" she asked.

"Will you just wait one minute?"

"No, I won't. You have one second to tell me why I shouldn't be going now. You're not my boyfriend and neither is he. Back off."

"No! You come here right now!"

Then Johnny stepped out of the car.

"Come with me," he said to his friend. You two stay in here," he told the two girls." Then they went up to Justin and to Blue.

"You don't ever take her anywhere!" Blue shouted in his face.

"I think the correct terminology is that you stay away from her and never come near her again," Johnny said, being cocky.

"You tell me to, and I won't do it." Then Blue walked over and grabbed Meganlynn by the arm.

"Ow!" she screamed.

"Get your hands off her!"

"No!"

"Get your hands off me!" Meganlynn shouted as she hit Blue in the head with her other elbow. "Kevin, get in the car, Johnny just drive."

"Okay." Then Kevin was in the car and Johnny was driving out of the driveway and onto the road. Justin and Blue were trying to follow, but they couldn't keep up on foot.

"She has to come back at some point," Blue said to Justin. "And until then, we will be waiting for her."

"Yes." Then Blue and Justin gave up and went back into camp.

"Who were those guys back there?" Johnny asked Meganlynn once they were out of earshot.

"The Justin guy was my ex-boyfriend. The guy who grabbed me was my sexual harasser."

"Oh. Well, how did you know to do that?"

"Well, someone saw the hurtful things that he was doing to me and told me that tonight was my night to shine and that I shouldn't let anyone take that away from me."

"They're right, you know?"

"It's my night to shine?"

"You're already shining."

"Good point," she joked, and they both laughed.

They all laughed and had fun for the rest of the night. Johnny, Tracey, Meganlynn, and Kevin all had fun when they went to dinner and then walked around the park. Finally, around eight o'clock, they went to the drive-in movie theater.

"Like the movie so far?" Johnny asked Meganlynn as they sat up on the top of the seats of his car while Kevin and Tracey were in the back seat.

"Yeah," she looked at him.

"You know, Kevin was supposed to borrow my car tonight and just leave me at home, or we had this deal worked out to the point where I was supposed to be the chauffer for the two of them, but I mean, now I don't have to. When I saw you sitting on my couch, I thought that your parents just died or something because I never thought I would ever see you again. Ask Kevin, I couldn't stop talking about you in the first place, and now that you're here, it's just like I can't help but see your face everywhere I look. I called your mom, and she had your phone number. She told me that you would probably be back in your cabin at five fifteen or something like that.

Once five fifteen rolled around, I called and you and your sweet, beautiful voice answered. I thought that I had just died when I asked you out, and you said that you would. I literally thought that I had just gone to heaven or was in a coma or something, but you're really here, with me, sitting in my car with me. You know, you really are the coolest girl that I have ever met in my life, and I doubt that I will ever meet anyone better than you ever again."

She blushed. "Johnny, you're so sweet. I love that about you. The truth of the matter is I had a bigger crush on you than you did on me when we first met. I was confused about what was ever going to happen in my life. I didn't know what kind of friends I had, or who my best friend really was. I loved the way that you looked, talked, sang, and the way that you looked at me. You were truly my knight in shining armor when I had met you. Then, the way you acted around Blue tonight showed me that you are still my knight in shining armor, and that I still love you even more than I did back then. When you called me, I was just as surprised as you were. To be truly honest, I had my night full of sorrow and depression and trying to forget everything that had been going on today."

"Well, Blue better keep his hands off you."

"How are you ever going to make sure that he knows that?"

"Oh, trust me; he'll get the picture sooner or later."

"I trust you, but do I want to know what you are going to do with him."

"It's not what I'm going to do; it's what God's going to do to him on the day of judgment."

"Good point." Part of her wanted to smile, but she knew that he was going to hell unless he repented.

"Yeah." Then he moved closer to her. She knew what he was doing, and it wasn't anything different than what her and Justin had done before. She missed Justin, but right now she couldn't even remember his name at all.

"Johnny?"

"Yeah?" He was now holding her close by the hip. Kevin and Tracey were asleep in the backseat.

"Have you ever even kissed a girl?"

"No, I've been saving it for this one special person."

"I have kissed a guy before but only one. I thought that I was never going to see you again, and I know that the one special person isn't me so I won't even bother." Then he did what she was not expecting him to do. He kissed her. After a few seconds, he was finally done, but Meganlynn had absolutely no objection to it happening for as long as it did.

"You are," he said as he pulled away.

"I was?"

"Duh, I just kissed you."

"Good point." Then, they sat there for a few more minutes.

"Looks like the night's over for us, Meganlynn."

"What?" asked Meganlynn who was just dozing off on his shoulder.

"I have to take you back."

"Please, no, I can stay with you. I have good reason to."

"How about tomorrow night I come and pick you up?"

"I'll have my stuff packed tonight."

"Okay, but I must warn you, it's family game night at the Gollingbird's."

"Does this face really look like it cares?"

"No."

Then he drove her back to the place that she hated the most, the place that was so revolting to her that every time she looked at it, she wanted to scream. She fell asleep on his shoulder on the way there. She had had such a good time with him that she did not want to forget it.

"Meganlynn, we're here."

She opened her eyes and there, before her, was the band camp. She was missing him and wanted more than anything for him to be a part of her life more than just the date.

"So does this means that we're dating?"

"Yeah, but what are we going to do when you go back?"

"I can be single every band camp that I come down."

"Just let me know when band camp is."

"Okay." Then, she was out of the car and so was he. He got out held her close and kissed her goodnight. They had her home ten minutes early so she had time to get to her cabin before anyone yelled at her.

"I love you," he said, holding her hand until she got into the camp where he couldn't go.

"Love you, too. Bye."

Then she was gone. He went back to his car and drove away, praying for her safety wherever she went inside the band camp.

Meganlynn turned and watched as the car headlights drove away. She missed him already. Her boyfriend, the one that never thought that she would ever see again; they were finally dating.

"Where were you?" asked a familiar voice from around the corner.

"I was out with a friend," she answered dreamily.

"Why were you out with him? Is he your boyfriend now or something?"

"Yeah, as matter of fact, Justin, he is. I don't think what we did is any of your business so just go away." Then, she walked toward her cabin. Blue jumped out and showed himself to her.

"What do you want, jerk?" she asked, her voice getting harder as the words came out of her mouth.

"I want you; we both do."

"Maybe, but this is already taken, sorry." She tried to walk by, but he grabbed her again.

"None of this," he said rubbing her up and then back down again, "is taken until you're dead."

"Well then, you'll just have to kill me," she said, having the most horrible feeling in her stomach.

"Trust me, I will."

"No, no, you won't." Then he struck her across the face and kicked her in the stomach. It hurt her more than any of the other beatings that she had taken from him. She hobbled back to her cabin, and thankfully, Alex was already asleep. She crawled into the covers and cried herself quietly to sleep.

CHAPTER 7

Meganlynn woke the next morning with bruises all over her body and she couldn't really move.

"Megan," her cabin partner said in a soft voice.

"Yeah?" Meganlynn asked as she woke.

"Why didn't you wake me when this happened?" she asked as she was looking around her bed.

"Because you were sleeping, and I wanted to lie down."

"Never think that if you have been beaten you are going to disturb me."

"Can I just stay here for the rest of the time?"

"Yeah, I'll go and tell someone about your little Blue ordeal."

"Okay." She was gone, leaving Meganlynn alone for a few seconds. Meganlynn had absolutely no idea that it was that long of a walk down to the field, but it was.

She sat up in her bed to find that she was staring right into the eyes of the boys that she never wanted to see again.

"What do you want?" she managed to speak out.

"You." Then they were both on her, raping her.

"Mr. Nolls! Please it's an emergency!" Alex yelled. "You have to help her!"

"Who? Who do I have help?" Mr. Nolls asked Meganlynn's cabin partner.

"Meganlynn. She's been beaten. I woke up this morning, and she wasn't awake. Her pillow was soaked in tears, and she had coughed-up some blood."

"Where is she?"

"She's up in our cabin."

"Who beat her?" He was now running.

"Blue, I think that she said that one of her ex-boyfriends was involved with it too, though."

"Okay, well let's get to her first."

She was lying there, alone. Justin and Blue had left. Justin had just done something that he could go to jail for, but he didn't care. He had wanted her in the same way and with the same intensity as Blue had. She hated them for it, too.

She got up, got dressed, grabbed her purse and car keys, and then walked out the back way to her car and drove away. Her eyes were blackened, and she was having a hard time seeing everything, but she was still capable of driving. She had hated Blue ever since he had stepped into her life a year ago and harassed her. She didn't hate Justin, but she knew that she should feel that way because of everything that they had just done to her. She put the CD back in and drove to a shopping center that was already beginning to crowd with people.

She sat down with her phone in hand and then called her parents from her phone. Her voice was shaky but she had to tell someone what had happened.

"Hello?" her mother's tired voice answered.

"Hi, Momma," answered her very shaky voice.

"Hi, honey, what's wrong?"

"Remember Blue?"

"Yeah, how could we forget him?"

"Well, you need to call Mr. Nolls and tell him that I am not coming back to band camp no matter what."

"Why?"

"Momma, Blue and Justin just raped me."

"They did what? I'm coming down there."

"Raped me! Blue has been beating me the whole time that I've been down here and—and now Blue finally did what he had been promising he was going to do and Justin just decided to join in."

"Okay, well go over to your aunt and uncle's house."

"I'll go to Johnny's house, he's my new boyfriend."

"Okay, honey, I'll call him and tell him that you're on your way and then. I'll let him know that we're going to be staying there for a few days."

"Okay."

"Honey," her mother's voice pleaded.

"Yeah." Meganlynn was trying not to cry or draw attention to her.

"Don't go anywhere without Johnny once you're with him, promise?"

"I promise."

"Okay. I'll make those two phone calls, and then I'll call you back."

"Okay, bye."

"Love you, Megan."

"Love you too, Momma," She hung-up the phone. She got up and walked back out to the car and then drove to Johnny's house.

"Hello?" Johnny answered his house phone sleepily.

"Hi. Johnny?" Meganlynn's mother replied.

"Yeah, but who is this?"

"This is Meganlynn's mother."

"Okay, is she okay?"

"You can ask her for me when she gets there, but she needs to stay with you for a couple of days or weeks or however long it takes okay?"

"Yeah, I'm pretty sure that my parents will be okay with it. It must be pretty major."

"She ran away from band camp."

"Oh, then it is pretty major."

"Yeah, it is."

"Okay, she can stay here."

"If your parents need to talk to me then just call me on this number okay?"

"Okay."

"She should be there in a few minutes, just take care of my baby, please."

"Trust me, I will."

"Thank you."

"Yeah," then they hung up the phone.

"Mom!" yelled Johnny.

"What Johnny?"

"Can Meganlynn stay here for a little while?"

"What?"

Johnny walked to his parents' room.

"Something happened to Meganlynn, and her mother just called and said she was on her way back here because she had to run away from her band camp for something."

"Yeah, she can stay for as long as she needs to."

"Okay, thanks." Then the door bell rung. *There she is,* he thought to himself. "I got it!" screamed Johnny as she ran down the stairs.

"Johnny," Meganlynn said coughing. She coughed up some more blood.

"Oh no," Johnny gasped.

"What?" she asked.

"I'll be right back down. Stay here."

"Okay?"

"Mom, Dad!"

Johnny ran back up the stairs and into his room to grab a pair of jeans, his keys, wallet, and shirt off of the floor.

"What Johnny?"

"I have to take Meganlynn to the hospital!"

"Why?"

"She just coughed up a little bit of blood. I got to take her."

"Okay." Then they went to the hospital.

"What happened to you? You look horrible."

"I know, Justin and Blue really did one over on me this time, didn't they?"

"Yeah, I'd say so."

"Why did they do this to me?"

"What did they do to you?"

"They raped me and beat me."

"Oh, well, make sure you tell the doctor that."

"Yeah, I will."

"Okay. So, are you okay?"

They turned into the hospital parking lot.

"Yeah, but I mean, I could barely move this morning."

"Okay, well stay there." He got out and came around to Meganlynn's door. He picked her up and carried her inside to the ER. "Nurse," he said.

"What's going on with her?"

"She's been raped and beaten today."

"Okay, I'll get the doctor straight away."

"I don't know if I can go in there with you, Meganlynn."

"Okay," she nodded her head along with her words. He hugged her close. "Ow!" she said.

"Does that hurt?"

"Yeah."

"Oh, I'm sorry."

"It's okay."

"The doctor will see you now. You can come back too."

"Okay." Then Johnny carried Meganlynn into the room and laid her out in the bed. They then wheeled her down to another room. He was allowed in here with her until the doctor got there.

"Okay, so what happened here?"

"She was raped and beaten."

"Okay, the police are going to want to talk to you, young lady."

"Doctor," Johnny started.

"Yes?"

"She also hurts when you hug her around her waist."

"Really?" he felt the area around her rib cage.

"Is she okay?"

"Are you down here on vacation or do you live here?"

"She's down here for band camp."

"Why can't she answer these questions?"

"She can barely talk, let alone move."

"Oh. Well the person that raped and beat her surely did a number on her then, didn't they?"

"Yeah, they did."

"Okay, well we won't have to get her into surgery to fix anything, and she'll be able to stay here to give her statement."

"Can I stay with her?"

"Are you the one that brought her in?" Johnny nodded his head. "Are her parents down here?" Johnny shook his head. "Then, yeah, you can stay."

"Thank you, Doctor."

"No problem."

"Do you want to call the police, Meg?" he asked her with pleading eyes, hoping that she would tell about the terrible beating that she had gone through.

"No," Meganlynn answered, even though she really wanted to. "I just want to go home."

"Why not?"

"I just want to go home, even though I have evidence against them. Maybe I'll take care of it when I get back in Michigan, but not down here."

"Meganlynn, this is what I say, get a lawyer and file charges. You know that you want to."

"Maybe, yes, Johnny, maybe I do, but maybe I don't want to do that to Justin."

"I know, but you have to tell someone that isn't a minor," Johnny answered getting a little irritated with Meganlynn's response.

"So what if I don't, Johnny? Are they going to throw me in jail? Hang me? They won't do any of that."

"Maybe not, but the police will be in here in a little while to get a police report."

"I still don't want to give them a statement."

"God will only let you die when he wants you back in heaven with him. If this guy wants you like this then he doesn't deserve you."

"Johnny, I know all of this!" Meganlynn pleaded with him. She didn't want to go back to band camp, and she did not want to have anyone bother her about it nor have anyone ask her about it. She needed that, but she also knew that she was never going to get it.

"Meg, I know that you know all of this, but you also have to understand that there are other reasons to turn Blue in other than for you. What if he decides to do this to someone else down the road?"

"Then they can take care of it."

"No, Meg! You can take care of it! You can take care of this, and you can show him that you are not going to be scared. You need to show him so he can't think, well he can think but—anyway, he more than likely won't threaten you with your life again if you tell more people, like the police, what had happened to you."

"Johnny." Meganlynn started sitting up in the hospital bed.

"What?" he asked, taking her hand and placing her hand in between his other hands.

"I am so scared that it isn't even funny. I mean, this guy raped me, and I want to tell more people about it, but you don't understand that I am so scared."

"I know that you are really scared, but you have to push through all of this and see all of the good you get out of telling the people that can help you. You need to tell someone that has the authority to help you."

"I know, Johnny, but please, quit harping on me about it."

"Never, Meganlynn, not until you tell the police everything that happened."

"Okay, I will tell them, but if I am killed then you are totally responsible for my death for making me tell the police the whole story."

"Meg, he could've killed you as it was. I'm honestly surprised that he didn't, considering what he did do to you."

"Well, it wasn't just him. I think that there was someone else there telling him not to kill me because he loved me way too much to do that, but it still makes me wonder. If Justin hadn't had been there would I even would be alive today?"

"Meg, don't think like that. You can't die. Well, not until God says that you can anyway."

"I know. He was there protecting me through all of this, too."

"I think he was."

"Yeah, not exactly that hard to figure out, huh?"

"No."

"How?"

"Well, you're alive for one thing."

"Good point." They both laughed at the uncomplicated joke that Johnny had just made. He was happy to see her laughing and smiling which he had not seen her do since she was out with him and his friends the night before. He liked to see her smile; he would miss her smile once she left Arizona and headed back to Michigan.

He knew that the next day and a half was going to be the last time that he would probably be the last time that he would see her until the next time she happened to be down in Arizona. He sat next to her bed as she spoke to him and tried to see the good in the fact that he most likely not to see her ever again. He looked back at the many memories that he had made with her from the very few hours he had spent with her. He was seriously going to miss her, but he knew that with her looks, she was bound to find someone else in no time at all. She did not need him, and he knew that.

She knew that she was going to miss him. She also knew that she was probably never going to see him again. She had gone through a hard time down here and Johnny was here for her through the very worst of it. Still, she needed a reason greater than being treated horribly, and he was there for her.

"Why are you scared of telling the police?" Johnny finally asked her after a few minutes of pure silence.

"I told you, if Blue ever found out that I told someone that he had done all of this stuff to me, then he would kill me just for telling you and my roommate. I just hope that by the time that he does find out that I told, he is long gone in a state prison and far away from me."

"You know that by the time he finds out, he will still be free and will still have people being able to do his bidding. You know this as well as the next guy that heard that threat."

"Yeah, but not everyone heard the threat. No one but Justin, Blue, and I heard the threat. I was really alone when he was threatening me."

"I knew that I should have walked you all the way to your cabin."

"How could you have known about what he was planning on doing?"

"I didn't, but trusting your gut is usually the thing that you're supposed to go by. Well, that and listening to God."

"Yeah, but, Johnny, I really need you to be right here with me on this. I need you here, protecting me."

"I think that God has that all figured out."

"That doesn't mean that I can't be scared."

"Keep your head down here on the earth instead of under it in fear; it seems fear is not from God."

"Well, I'm not exactly in hell. No, that was last night."

"Maybe not, but Meg, I'm not getting into get into it with you."

A knock came to the door. There were two police officers standing on the other side of the door. Meganlynn squinted at the mere sight of them; she really did not want to let them in.

"Want me to let them in Meg?" Johnny asked her walking over to the door.

"No."

Johnny turned the doorknob. "Too bad." He opened the door and let the two police officers in and her mother in.

"Hello ma'am," the first police officer said.

"Hello," Meganlynn answered back in a lowered voice.

"My name is Sergeant Billard," the first police officer said. He was tall, with dark hair and brown eyes. He was also thin and wore the police uniform very well. "And this," he said, pointing to the other police officer on his left, "is Sergeant Holgrind. We're here to take your case."

"How did you find out that I needed the police?" Meganlynn asked him.

"We received a call about an hour ago."

"Really?" Meganlynn asked as she looked over to Johnny who just shrugged his shoulders.

"We are here for you to file a police report, ma'am," the police officer said once again.

"Well, I don't quite know if I really want to file a police report."

"Ma'am, it would be a very wise decision. If the same person were to ever do this to someone else ever again, then we have this as evidence against him."

"He's not going to do this to anyone else."

"Why is that?"

"That is because he's still after me."

"Then, you really need to tell us everything that had happened."

"I don't know, he—he," She paused. Meganlynn could not help it; she needed to re-think everything that had been made for her. She needed to re-think everything that had been said to her. She needed to think about her life, friends, family, and priorities. She needed to think about all of these things.

"He threatened her," Johnny finished for her after a few seconds of thinking to herself.

"Johnny," Meganlynn pleaded with him.

"Meganlynn, whether you're dead or alive, they were going to find out. They were going to find out if you were dead because I would've been the one that called the police in the first place. Even if they hadn't found out, and you were still alive I would've been the one to tell them because I owe it to you!"

"Fine," Meganlynn answered.

"Ma'am are you going to tell us what happened?" the police officer asked once she and Johnny were done with their little misunderstanding.

"Yes," she answered.

Meganlynn told them everything. She told them how he had harassed her the previous year, and how he had started back up this year. She told him everything that had been going on between her and Justin. How he had helped Blue keep her there the previous night and how he was there when everything that had happened. How he had tried to beg her to go back with him, and how she refused him.

"Ma'am, this is what really happened?" the police officer asked after she had finished her story.

"Yes," Meganlynn answered with a weary voice that sounded as though she was going to cry at any point.

"Are you going to file charges against these two men?"

"What would that mean for Blue and Justin?" Johnny asked.

"It means that she can appear in court, and then, the judge or jury can decide if they did it or not."

"Can I pursue charges with one person, but yet drop the charges on the other person?" Meganlynn asked the police officer after she had finished thinking about if she had really wanted to charge Blue and Justin.

"Sorry, ma'am, but you must charge both of them because they committed the crime together."

"Okay, then, I don't want to file charges against them."

"Meganlynn, you need to have the charges pressed!" Johnny screamed while having a tear of fear come to his eye.

"Honey, you have to," her mother begged her, stroking her hair.

"Johnny, do you even know how scared I am? Do you even care?" Meganlynn asked him once the tear had finished rolling down his cheek and fell onto her hand.

"Meganlynn, I care more than anything about you, that's why I'm telling you that you need to press charges."

"Quit telling me that. I know everything that happened, I know every way that Blue threatened me, and everything that he loved about me. I knew everything that he thought about me, everything."

"Well, everything that he did to you is everything that he needs pressed against him. You need to have every charge pressed on him and Justin that you can possibly get. You need everything that would be evidence that you need in court to put them both away."

"Still, Johnny! You need to be hearing me! Johnny, please!"

"Meganlynn! You need to get your head out of the clouds! You need to be the normal Meganlynn that I know instead of this girl that has her head in the clouds! Please Meganlynn, press charges against them."

"No."

"Well, we're going to go. It's our dinner break, and I don't think that this young lady wants to press charges against them from what she has been saying. Have a good day." Johnny ran out the door after the two police men as they ran toward their car.

"Excuse me," he started, getting one of the police officer's attention, "can I file charges against him?"

"Only if you witnessed it."

"Oh," Johnny answered with his face seeming to fall.

"Good day, sir." Then the other police officer walked away and Johnny went back into the room with Meganlynn.

"Why won't you press charges?"

"Would you?"

"Yeah, how badly did they threaten you?"

"My life, but that's not the reason that I won't press charges."

"Then what is?" Johnny was now almost yelling at Meganlynn for making her decision of not pressing charges.

"I don't want Justin to have this on his record."

"He was there and you still didn't report it, Meg. He deserves it more than most people do!" He was yelling at her.

"Stop yelling at me. I need to think. Is he actually responsible for this?"

"Well, I didn't see him running to get help."

"Yeah, I know that he didn't. I know that he didn't run for help. He helped—Blue." Her face fell. She had known that she was there and so were Blue and Justin. She had not realized that Justin had actually helped Blue in the middle, and he had actually done it.

"Do you want to press charges now?"

"Yeah. Why did he do this to me?"

"I don't know. Probably because he's a loser and he knows it."

"Thank you, Johnny."

"Yeah, anytime."

"Uh, I'm so stupid to not press charges against them."

"Well, there's still time."

"I know."

"Okay, but if you don't, I'll come and get you personally."

"I believe you."

"Okay." Her head was now on his chest, and he was holding her close so she would feel protected. The plane ride home was going to be stressful enough for her, but she needed time to recover and time to stay here. She needed not to return to the place that she was at that time in her life. He knew what she needed. The next day was the day that they would have to be free from everything that she had known. He knew exactly where he was going to take her tomorrow.

CHAPTER 8

The final day that had been given to go shopping went great for Meganlynn and the rest of the group. Blue had not bothered her all day long and she was very happy about that, but that was because he could not seem to find her where Johnny had taken her.

Meganlynn stayed with Johnny's family for the night. She did not want to go back to the cabin where her pillow was all bloody from that night, but she had gone back and packed her things before she had left to go shopping. She had people starring at her and whispering behind her back, but she had expected that since she had been the person to run away from the camp.

Instead of giving everyone the pleasure of her responding to their whispers, she would just ignore them because most of the time they just ignored her anyway. She heard every little thing that they were saying about her as she walked in and back out.

"Look, there's the girl that ran away," someone would whisper. They really didn't care whether or not they were hurting her feelings. And they really didn't know what had happened that night. Her friends tried to talk to her, but Meganlynn could not take hearing it any longer, and she left.

Johnny took her and her friends to the largest mall that he could find. He had the most fun with all of them because he got to hear stories about Meganlynn from her friends that had been around her for most of her life. She needed, more than anything, to just stay down there and not have to go back to the cabin. She knew that she did not have to go back to the cabin, but she did have to board the plane the very next day.

The day had gone well. It was the best day that Meganlynn had had since she had been down there. She was having a ball, that is, she was until it was time to take her friends back to their camp site. Meganlynn would not go back into the camp, she stayed Johnny's house now. Everything had happened so fast that she had not had time for fun with her friends. Now, was the day that she had to return to all of it. With a good-bye and a thank you to the family that had been so kind to her, she was off with Johnny to get to the airport to go home. Her parents were going to give her the same speech that Johnny had tried to give her when she was back in the hospital. She was prepared for that, but she was not prepared for what was going to happen when she finally got to the airport.

"Meganlynn." Johnny started out once they had finally both gotten into the car.

"Yeah?" Meganlynn responded, knowing what he was about to do.

"You know that I won't be able to fly to Michigan every weekend to see you."

"I know, but I mean, why are we torturing ourselves like this?"

"Because we may be in love with each other."

"I'll make sure that I'm single every time that band camp is down here," Meganlynn offered. They knew that this long-distance relationship would never work between them.

"Just give me a call before you come down, and I will be single, too," Johnny's eyes were still filling with tears. *Did he truly want to have forever and always? Yes. Did he truly need her like he felt that he needed her? Yes, and he knew this was a fact. Were they meant to be together? Yes. Did he know how to tell her? No.*

They grabbed her things out of the back of his car and made their way into the airport. Johnny was allowed to walk into check-in with her but anything further than that was off-limits. She knew that the time would come when she would have to go through check-in and have to say good-bye to him. Did she want to? No. She knew all of the things that Johnny knew about the two of them, but just like him, she did not know how to tell him how she truly felt. The check-in went faster than anyone thought, and it was time for Johnny and Meganlynn to say good-bye to one another. Blue was waiting on the other side of the gate for Meganlynn, looking at her as though he wanted her on a platter right in front of her.

Johnny knew that this moment was coming just as much as Meganlynn had known that it was coming. They both knew that it was way too soon for either of them. Once they had come to the check-in, Johnny and Meganlynn then knew that it was time for their good-byes.

"Until next year," Johnny said, looking at Meganlynn one last time.

"E-mail and call? Promise?" she asked him as she moved an inch farther in line.

"Yes, come here," he held her once, even closer and tighter, until the line moved forward, and they both would move in order to keep the people behind them happy.

"Bye, Johnny," Meganlynn whispered in his ear.

"Yeah, good-bye." He pulled her into one more kiss that she would remember until next year. Meganlynn picked-up her things and went through the check-in and then was gone from his sight.

"Meganlynn," a familiar voice came. She knew exactly who it was and what he was waiting for.

"What Blue?" she asked as she walked farther and farther away from him down the hallway that held the airport. She missed Justin being on her side. She still felt like the Lord was with her protecting her, and she also felt as though Satan was right on her back, seeing her every move and giving everything he had to just make her life a disaster.

Johnny missed her as well. He missed the touch of her hand and the smell of the body lotion that she had been wearing ever since it had all happened. He missed every little thing about her, other than Blue stalking her that is, and he could not wait for the next year and for the first time that she would call and then write him. He could not wait for her to send him all of her books so then he could read them and tell her what he thought of them. He missed her more than anything.

"Well," Blue started as he and Justin walked toward her. "I thought that it would be nice if we all had lunch together."

"Why?"

He looked her up and then back down again. "So we can get to know each other a little bit better."

"I don't want to get to know you better."

"You know that I want to and that all I care about is the care and well-being of you," Blue's teeth were gritted together and Meganlynn could tell that he was mad.

"What do you want from me?"

"Everything."

"How? You already raped me. Have you punished me enough already? "

"Yes, I had to punish you."

"Then leave me alone."

"No. If I was done punishing you, then I wouldn't be here right now talking to you."

"Then get the point."

"Never will you be able to get rid of me, Meganlynn. Even if you go off to collage, I will still be there." Blue had her cornered against the wall of the airport. They may have been ordered to be there an hour earlier than the plane was going to be there, but that was so everyone would get their shopping stuff all done. Meganlynn knew that she had to find one of her friends or a security guard.

"Blue, leave me alone please," she begged.

"No, I love you too much." He stroked her face. She started to cry harder than she ever had before.

"Let me go." She stepped away from him and ran to the bathroom until the plane came.

An hour had almost passed when Meganlynn came out of the bathroom to try to find the gate that she was to go into for the plane. She walked into the gate with the rest of the band looking at her as if she had done something wrong. She knew that everyone was thinking different things about her. She wanted everything to stop: the whispers, the looks, and all of the thoughts.

"Look there's the girl that ran away", she heard one girl whisper.

"Really? Well, why did she run away?" the girl sitting next to her asked.

"I think it's because she wasn't up for the challenge."

Meganlynn just walked on by and tried not to pay attention to the other people who whispered as she walked by until she got to her friends.

Once she got to her friends, Lizzie, Morgan, and Taylor were all sitting next to each other with one seat empty for Meganlynn to sit in. They knew that Meganlynn would want to sit next to them after everything that had happened. As she walked by to her seat they all stood up and hugged her making Meganlynn twinge little bit from the pain.

"Hey guys," she said, sitting down as her voice was still shaking and hard to understand. She missed everyone and everything about every little detail of spending time with her friends.

"Meg!" Lizzie, Morgan, and Taylor all shouted at different times, one right after the other.

"Hey," she said, sitting down.

"Why did you run away?" Lizzie asked. Meganlynn knew that someone was going to ask that question.

"Because of Blue." Her voice was an inch away from crying.

"What did he do?" Morgan asked right after Meganlynn had gotten done saying why she had left.

"He raped me," she whispered and put her head in her hands. While the rest of her friends just sat there with their mouths wide open.

"He did what?" Taylor asked with a very surprised look on her face. She knew what she had said, but she was very surprised about what had happened.

"He raped me."

"Well, he was being nice wasn't he?" Morgan said sarcastically.

"Yeah, and you want to know the worst part about it, though?" Meganlynn asked as she sat with her friends in the waiting room.

"What?" all three of them asked almost like one after another.

"Justin was standing right there watching."

"He was what?" Lizzie asked as all of the other girls' mouths were dropped to the ground.

"He was standing right there, watching." Meganlynn was trying not to cry as she looked at the ground seeing everything that had happened that night flashing through her mind. Tears naturally ran down her face whenever she seemed to think about that night alone. She was crying now, not loudly but silently.

She stared at the ground for a few moments until the plane was finally called to board. As usual, Morgan, Lizzie, and Taylor were surrounding her. She was crying and the flight attendants were always asking her what was wrong when she got onto the plane. She couldn't tell them, not yet at least.

Once the plane was up in the air, Meganlynn was writing a story on what she had been going through the past week. She was the main person for someone to go to if they needed to talk about their problems and issues, but Meganlynn could never find anyone to talk to about her own problems and concerns. Johnny had been the only person that would listen during the time that they were down there in Arizona.

Meganlynn was sitting next to Lizzie with Taylor and Morgan behind them and two other people that Meganlynn could not see in front of them. Meganlynn started to scan the plane. *Where were Blue and Justin?* She thought to herself. She was scared that she couldn't see them. They might have been in front of her, and that, to her, was the scariest thing in the world to her: sitting behind the two guys that had raped her.

Meganlynn had finally started to write again. She wrote about everything that had happened to her every day of that past week and also every day of that past year when he had harassed her to the breaking point.

She came out of her "own little place" once one of her friends tapped her on the shoulder and had made her stop writing. She noticed that she was on the last page of her notebook. She was surprised; she had only been writing for three hours. She normally didn't write for three hours straight, but she wasn't normally this upset about something either. She was confused and hurt. Once her friends made her stop, her hand hurt more than anything. She wiggled her wrist back and forth in order to try to make it feel a little bit better.

"I would ask you why you are crying, but you know, I already know why," Morgan said, looking at Meganlynn. Tears had flooded the pages so bad that they looked even more fragile than the Declaration of Independence.

"Yeah," Meganlynn said under her breath, just loud enough for Lizzie to hear her. The tears really started to run down her cheek, and her normal voice was now the pitch of the highest pitch they could do.

"Meg, only dogs can hear you sweetie," Lizzie told her, placing her hand on her shoulder.

"Sorry, but it's just that—it's just—it's just that I am so scared."

"We know." Taylor placed her hand on Meganlynn's shoulder too and looked back up to Lizzie with what seemed to be a tear in her eye.

"Girls." Lizzie started off looking at all the girls other than Meganlynn. "I have to go to the bathroom."

"Yeah, and quiet hour starts soon," Taylor said, sitting back in her seat.

"Which means that we can't talk anymore and that we also have to try to sleep a little bit," Morgan added.

"Ding!" The girls looked up to the front of the plane to see the little light on to show that it was quiet time and that passengers were not allowed to move around. Well, the only reason that they were allowed to move was to go to the bathroom. Lizzie was still in the bathroom by the time that Morgan and Taylor had fallen asleep from the pure exhaustion of the day of shopping and from band camp. Meganlynn was still wide-awake and thinking and re-seeing everything that had happened. She cried, but she didn't mean to. She actually just wanted to have the visions gone from her head.

Her mind trembled inside of her trembling body. She shook while she sat there and waited for Lizzie to come back from the bathroom. She knew that she was not dead, but she also knew that she was not coming back from the bathroom. Then, her worst nightmare happened; Blue came and sat there and then started to talk to her, again.

"Hey baby," he said as he sat down. He put his hand on top of Meganlynn's leg just like he had many times before. Meganlynn was finally tired of all of the crap that Blue was trying to pull on her. She then picked-up her Bible and then began to read once again from it.

"Excuse me," she said as she turned the pages to the one that she wanted. She finally found Revelation eleven and began to read it silently.

"What are you reading?" He then began to stroke her hair as if she had been his own personal prostitute.

"The Two Witnesses," she answered. She refused to look at him for even a second. She knew that just looking at him would be a huge pain because of all of the things that he had done to her in the past week.

"What does it say?"

"Why should I tell you?" His mouth was now on her neck, breathing down it. Her hair was standing on end because she was so scared. She peeked at the aisle-way to see if Lizzie was anywhere to be seen, but she had no such luck. Blue was right next to her, and she had to deal with it as she had so many times before.

"Because if you don't, I may just have to go back on my word of not killing you." His hands moved up on her legs. "This is your fault, and you know it," he whispered in her ear.

"Okay, fine, I will tell you everything that this says."

"I thought that you would see it my way."

"I was given a message stick like a rod, and I was told, 'Go and measure the temple of God and the alter, and count the people worshiping there. But do not measure the yard outside the temple. Leave it alone, because it has been given to those who are not God's people. And they will trample on the holy city for forty-two months. And I will give one thousand two hundred and sixty days, and they will be dressed in rough cloth to show their sadness.'" Tears were running down Meganlynn's face like a river in the rain on a windy day. "These two witnesses are the two olive trees and the lamp stands that stand before the Lord of the earth. And if anyone tries to hurt them, fire comes from their mouths and kills their enemies. And if anyone tries to hurt them in whatever way, in that same way that person will die. These witnesses have the power to stop the sky from raining during the time they are prophesying. And they have the power to make the waters become blood, and they have the power to send every kind of trouble to the earth as many times as they want.

"When the two witnesses have finished telling their message, the beast that comes up from the bottomless pit will fight a war against them. He will defeat them and kill them. The bodies of the two witnesses will lie in the street of the great city where the Lord was killed. This city is named Sodom and Egypt, which has a spiritual meaning. Those from every race of people, tribe, language, and nation will look at the bodies of the two witnesses for three and one-half days, and they will refuse to bury them. People who live on earth will rejoice and be happy because these two are dead. They will send each other gifts, because these two profits brought much suffering to those who live on earth.

"But after three and one-half days, God put the breath of life into the two prophets again. They stood at their feet, and everyone who saw them became very afraid. Then the two prophets heard a loud voice from heaven saying, 'Come up here!' And they went up into heaven in a cloud as their enemies watched.

"In the same hour there was a great earthquake, and a tenth of the city was destroyed. Seven thousand people were killed in the earthquake, and those who did not doe were afraid and gave glory to the God of heaven.

"The second trouble is finished. Pay attention: The third trouble is coming soon." Meganlynn took a breath and then looked back at Blue. She had been saying all of this stuff and secretly wishing that he was going through it at the moment. She was hopefully going to over-come this terrible wish. "Am I done?"

"Well, I kind-of want my seat back," Lizzie said as she stood with her arms crossed and her hip cocked. She held her defeating gaze as Blue got out of her seat and off Meganlynn.

"Well um…" He mimicked back to her still having his hands on Meganlynn. "I guess you have to find a different one then don't you?"

"Does it look like she really wants that?" Lizzie asked pointing at Meganlynn, wondering what was really going through her head at this moment.

"I don't know, does it?" he asked looking back at Meganlynn.

"Oh, please," Lizzie shot back.

"I really don't care." Meganlynn lied with a tear coming down her eyes. She was deathly scared and unable to say anything other than that. It was the first thing and the only thing that came to her mind when she was confronted with the question. She was heart-broken as her friend looked at her as if she was a chicken and then walked away. She knew what she gotten herself into.

Maybe I said the right thing, she thought to herself. *After all, I do deserve it for letting it go on for so long. I probably brought it on all on my own. I deserve this, everything.*

"Would you like to read to me again?" Blue asked Meganlynn as she closed her Bible.

"No, I honestly wouldn't. I want to have a little bit of time to myself to think things over."

"Fine, but I get to keep my hands on you all the time, don't I?"

"Do I have a say?"

"No!" he whispered in her ears. Meganlynn took a deep breath and let the tears fall from her face onto her lap.

Blue had his hands on her all the way home. At this point he had one hand on her hands making her unable to write or do any of the other things that she wanted to do to get her anger out. He was hurting her, her hand felt as if her hand was going to fall off. But yet she couldn't help herself any. She couldn't even try. The other hand was placed heavily on her leg to make her even more and more uneasy. She was officially scared.

All Meganlynn could do was sit there and think. Her hands were not free from Blue's grip on them. All she wanted to do was write, it was the only way that she knew how to get her emotions out from having all of the memories that she had been having. The images in her mind flashed back and forth from one image to the next in chronological order. She had her by the leg and by the hands.

Scared as she was, she then looked at her notebook that only had about fifteen pages left. The seventy-page notebook was sitting on the table behind the seat. She reached to for the notebook and grabbed it. Then she grabbed her pen and then began to then write things down. She wrote slowly, but she wrote it down.

She wrote, and wrote, and Blue never woke. He was holding her and touching her inappropriately, but she was happy that she could write all of her feelings down on the paper instead of thinking for the rest of the time about what he was doing and what he had done to her. The pen flew across the page and went to the next page just as soon as she had flipped the previous page. The plane ride may have almost been over, but Meganlynn was in for a rough night.

Practices every other night would soon follow the turmoil of band camp and make her want to die even more, but she would not. She knew that this was only a phase that she was going through in order to have all of the information to sue him and make him pay when she went to court for it. She was going to take him to court; she did not know how or when, she just knew that she was taking him to court.

Then, the flight attendant looked at where Blue's hands were placed on Meganlynn, she wondered why he was allowed to place one hand on her boob and the other in between her legs. She had absolutely no idea that Meganlynn was being put through torture.

"Excuse me, ma'am," the flight attendant whispered to Meganlynn. She was leaning over Blue, and she was also waking Blue up from the sleep that he was in the middle of.

"Yes?" Meganlynn answered.

"Is it okay with you that he touches you like this?" Meganlynn's face told the whole story. She was very scared. If she said no, Blue would wake, but if she said yes, everyone around her would think that she was in-love with Blue and not able to love anyone else.

"It's fine," Meganlynn lied.

"Ma'am, I'm sorry to come into your life like this, but you don't look very happy like this."

"I really don't care as long as he doesn't wake. He gets upset and cranky and I really don't want to sit next to someone like that for the next three hours."

"Ma'am, I'm sorry, but we only have one hour left."

"Oh, but still, I don't want to wake him."

"Okay, I am going to have to tell your band teacher."

"Fine, I'll make him move."

"Okay, thank you, ma'am." Then she left. Meganlynn kept her promise and then moved Blue's hands from where they were.

Blue moved a little bit from where they were, but not enough to make a difference. She then moved his hands a little bit further away, and he began to wake.

"What did you get me up for, honey?" He woke to say as she began to move his hands farther and farther away from where they originally were on her.

"I didn't mean to. I just wanted to have a little bit of freedom."

"Well, then why didn't you just ask?"

"You really would've moved your hands away from where they were?"

"No, but it never hurts to ask."

"Wow." She sat there and leaned her head back as he placed his hands back on her hands again not letting her do anything but sit there and think about whatever he was doing to her at that very moment.

All she could possibly think about was what he was doing to her at that exact moment. She had always hated him, even when they were little kids. He was her natural enemy and was never liked by her parents or any of her family members.

Blue still held her so she could not move. Meganlynn was a very laid-back person, but when you got her angry, she could be one of the meanest people ever.

A small, simple, little tear then fell from her check onto Blue's arm. He was now fully awake and then he turned back around so he was facing fully toward Meganlynn and began to talk to her.

"Why are you crying, sweetheart?" he asked her. He sounded like he was all simple and sweet.

"Nothing," Meganlynn spat back out. She turned away from him and stared out of the window.

"Look at me!" he shouted in her ear in the worst sort of voice ever.

"No," Meganlynn stated and still stayed facing away from him.

"Look, you really don't have a choice. You are either going to look at me or you're not. Get over it." He grabbed her face and made her look at him.

"No, I believe that I am going to the bathroom, if you don't mind." The look on her face was a horrified look. She then got up walked over him and then started off to the bathroom that was, until halfway in the aisle way when he grabbed her leg, making her fall down in the aisle.

Of course, as she went down, she screamed and got back up, and gave him an extremely dirty look. She was then off to the bathroom.

She got in and sat down. She sat down and cried for everything that had been going on. Soon enough, there was a knock at the door.

"Someone's in here!" she shouted as she cried and held her knees close to her chest.

"Let me in!" She recognized the voice that she had been hearing the whole time of the plane ride. She was scared. She knew that she almost had to let him in; she also knew that she had to stick up for herself. She stared at the door, while Blue tried his hardest to break it down. She knew that, to everyone else, she was invisible, and she was going to be raped and beaten just as she was at band camp and before. She had already been sexually harassed by this boy, and now, once again, he had started it. Then again, she was going to be raped, and it hopefully was not going to be something worse than that involved. He broke down the door.

"Well, that was rude!" he yelled, slapping her across the face. No one had heard him.

"Well, I was going to the bathroom," she stated back as she was looking at the ground in pure pain and torture.

"I've already seen you naked! Nothing new to me!" Meganlynn continued to cry harder and harder as he yelled at her more and more.

"I don't care." She then looked up to see his face as he stared at her harder and harder as the stare of death was planted right in his eyes.

"You will care when I get done with you!" he then began to beat her. First, he punched her in the mouth, and then harder and harder in her face. Having braces, it meant that she had the marks of her braces imbedded in her lips. He then moved back down farther and farther on her body. He then beat her harder and harder as he went farther and farther down her body. He hit her harder as he beat her closer and closer to her stomach. Blood started to come back up her throat and then onto the floor of the bathroom. He then was done.

"There, that serves you right." Once more he kicked her in the stomach. She lay there, dying on the ground. There were people out in the plane area and no one had asked where she was quite yet. Things were beginning to become very strange.

I am so invisible to the naked eye, Meganlynn thought to herself. *But, maybe I deserved this. I did deserve this. I am a horrible person. I did this to myself. If I had truly wanted this to stop, then I would've been able to. I guess I wanted it to keep on going. That's why. That's why it didn't stop.*

She sat and cried on the ground. No one knew nor cared where she was. All of her friends were asleep in their chairs and they were in their normal enough to keep in their own little private worlds and their own little silly dreams while Meganlynn was sitting on the bathroom floor, dying.

Meganlynn heard footsteps, a guy's footsteps. She figured that Blue was coming back for round two. She breathed heavy and prayed silently that God would just take her life right there and then. She was scared that Blue was back there for her, finally. Thankfully, she was wrong.

He came to the doorway of the bathroom and found her lying on the ground. He stared for a minute and walked up to her. He bent down and lifted her head so he could see her eyes.

"Meganlynn, what happened to you?" he asked.

"Justin?" Meganlynn asked as she opened her eyes from being closed for the time that she thought Blue was on his way back.

"Yes," he said. He held her close to his chest.

"Justin, help me," she cried.

"I will, I promise. Who did this to you?" he asked as tears fell down her face.

"Thank you," she forced out. She had had so much taken away from her already that she could not take it anymore. She had to have people be there for her. She needed everyone to know who had in fact done this to her. She needed *everyone* to know.

He walked out of the room to get help.

"I'll be right back," he told her as he went out the door.

"Okay." Meganlynn was right back where she was. She was back on the ground, suffering once again. She wanted everything to stop. She wanted the horrible life here on earth to be over with and to just go up to Heaven.

Finally she heard footsteps again, male footsteps. She looked up with all of her might to find out who was standing in the doorway. She was terrified. She was lying there, looking up at Blue.

Blue stood there, in the doorway of the bathroom where Meganlynn was laying. She was trying to move away as fast as she could. She looked him right in the eyes.

"Hello," he said as he walked over to her.

"Hi," she said moving away from him.

"Hello, once again." He moved closer until he reached her and, once she could not move any further, he bent down so he was right next to her.

"Stay away from me," she whispered. She felt as though she was pleading for her life.

"No, I don't think that I will." He moved closer to her.

"Help!" she squeaked, but then was forced to stop when he kicked her in the throat. Justin, Mr. Nolls, Lizzie, Morgan, Taylor, and one flight attendant were all running to the bathroom where Meganlynn was laying, helpless on the ground.

"No one's going to help you now," Blue told her after he had kicked her. Justin, Lizzie, Morgan, and Taylor ran faster to the bathroom where she was while the others ran a bit slower.

"Justin!" she tried to scream in her hoarse voice, but it was not any use. No one was able to hear her now; it was almost as if she were dead and unable to say anything about what had happened that night.

"Blue! Get off her!" Justin screamed when he got to the doorway he pulled Blue off Meganlynn. Lizzie, Morgan, and Taylor were on the ground helping Meganlynn to sit up as she was laying now flat on the ground. They attended to her while the rest then went to get Blue out of the room.

Meganlynn was placed next to Justin until the plane was landed. She didn't have a want or a need to believe that Justin had done anything to her. She couldn't remember anything that had happened that night. He was supposed to help her off the plane, onto the stretcher, and to the hospital. She knew that it was all, finally, over. She knew that one way or another, Blue was never going to see the light of day again.

She finally got the rest that she had needed and wanted. It only took four hours to fly from Arizona back to Michigan, and three of those four hours had passed. She got to sleep for the last fifty minutes with her head on Justin's shoulder. She dreamt of last year, the good parts. She had many reasons not to trust him. He had been there when Blue was raping her, but then again with the performance in the bathroom, how could she not trust him? He was the person that she loved, and she wanted more than anything to trust him again.

"I'll never let you go," Justin whispered to her as they were all waiting for Mr. Nolls to come from the high school. "You'll stay right here in my arms."

"I know." Meganlynn snuggled up to him even more. She let him hold her and love her. She went through all of the good memories with him, everything that they had done together. She needed all of the good memories that she had left because she felt so helpless sitting next to Justin. Justin seemed to be okay to Meganlynn, but there was something about him that just did not seem right.

Her friends all passed by the seats to make sure that she was alive and breathing. Blue was up with the pilot and Mr. Nolls. The flight attendant made her routine visits while she was going back and forth to the different seats. Through all of it, Meganlynn slept. Justin was right next to her watching her sleep to make sure that she did not die. He also wanted to say some things that he wanted to tell her while she could not hear him.

"Please prepare for landing," the flight attendant said, and Justin had to wake Meganlynn.

"Meg," he said touching her. She needed to put her seatbelt on.

"What?" she asked sleepily.

"You need to put your seatbelt on, baby."

"Okay." She got back up and put it on. Meganlynn was now in Justin's hands for safety, and he, at least, knew it. As the plane landed, he got ready to carry Meganlynn and have his two other friends carry both of their carry on luggage. When the plane landed, he knew that he had to get Meganlynn off the plane.

He carried her off. He hurried to the helicopter that would soon hold Meganlynn's dying body.

"Here she is!" he yelled once he had got the chance to run off the plane and place Meganlynn on the stretcher.

"Okay!" he heard a paramedic say.

"Justin," she whispered. He then held her hand.

"Please, Meganlynn, don't die."

"No, dying would be too easy." A smile came on her face. She was going to live. He then watched her go when they rolled her away and she went to the hospital.

He saw Blue was coming off the plane and going with the police. Lizzie, Morgan, and Taylor were looking for either Meganlynn or her parents to see what had happened to her. They never thought of going to Justin, she hadn't talked to him since they had broken-up. Then, Meganlynn was suddenly gone from his sight.

"You moron," he said as he walked to Blue who was standing in the doorway of the police car.

"How am I such a moron?" Blue asked as if Justin had had something to do with this the whole time.

"You raped her."

"Point being?"

"You raped her!"

"Yeah, and there's a problem with that?"

"There's a huge problem with that!"

"What did I do to the poor little rich girl that you didn't?"

"You beat, raped, and threatened her. I never did any of that!"

"Wow, now denial. Tut, tut, tut, tut, no one knows what to do with you there Justin."

"I don't care. You come within five hundred feet of her, and I'll call the police."

"I am in police custody right now, and I will have to be there for the trial since you will most likely be pressing charges against me. She dropped them the first time."

"That was her decision, I'm sure she's going to want to press them now that her parents are there by her side."

"She'll just drop them all again."

"She won't have a choice with all of her family and friends behind her."

"I don't think she's going to have all of her friends by her side."

"She'll have most of them by her side."

"Guess who she was going to date and has moved up here?"

"I know that she misses that Johnny guy, and I know that she knows a lot of people."

"Guess what: She still loves him."

"She hasn't exactly committed her love to me."

"Still, aren't you at least a little bit in love with her still?"

"Yes, but I betrayed her. I was talking to you. I hurt her more than anything."

"And you finally figured out why, wow even I knew why she dumped you."

"I'm done." He shut the door in his face. Blue was driven away by two police officers that were taking him to the county jail house.

CHAPTER 9

The paramedics rushed Meganlynn into the emergency room. She was hurting more than she had ever had before.

"How is she doing?" Justin asked walking into the waiting room.

"We don't know yet. She's in the operating room," her mother cried. "Who did this to her anyway?"

"Blue, he did everything."

"And you were where?" asked her father, sternly.

"We broke up. I was talking to Blue. She was so upset that she broke-up with me. I was surprised, and yet mad that she dumped me."

"Well, why weren't there to protect her? Why were you not there when she needed you? Where was your head?" He began shouting at Justin.

"I wasn't there because someone else was. I was off hanging out with my friends when she needed me. My head was somewhere off in the clouds thinking about how much I loved her and how much I wanted her back. I know that I was wrong."

"You were really wrong to do that!" His wife then put her hand on his arm to tell him that this was not the place for everything to happen.

"I know that I was being stupid. I knew that we were going to get back together, and I was sad when we stopped going out. I wish that I would not have been there talking to Blue, but I was. I hope that I get the chance to get to tell her that myself."

"I think you will. I think you will get to tell her that line."

"Blue really did a number on her, sir," he answered, scared.

"I know. Hope that you can tell her that, and if she doesn't make it, then you can make sure that she knows when you are saying good-bye to her at her funeral. And know that I will partly blame you for this happening to her if she dies. Especially since you were not there for her when all of this was being done."

"Okay, sir." They were sitting down while they waited for the doctor to come back and tell them what was going on with Meganlynn. They waited for about three hours before another word was said. Many doctors came out and then left with other families. Finally, Meganlynn's doctor came out.

"She seems to be all right. We want her to stay over-night and see how she reacts to the medications," the doctor told them.

"Can we see her? Is she awake yet?" her mother asked in a panicking voice.

"She's not quite awake yet, but she will be soon," the doctor explained as she wrote something down on the clipboard that she was carrying.

"I don't care, can we see her?" Meganlynn's mother asked.

"Yes, you may see her, but only you three."

"Thank you." Justin walked down the hallway and into the room that Meganlynn was in.

Meganlynn's mother and father ran over to her daughter and hugged her. Justin just stood and looked at her when she slept.

After they were done, they sat in the chairs for hours waiting for Meganlynn to wake. She was asleep and everyone was getting hungry.

"Justin," her mother started.

"Yeah?" he responded.

"Will you stay here with Meganlynn while we go and get food that he can actually eat?"

"I will."

"Thank you." Meganlynn's parents walked out the door and went to get food. He just wanted to be there when Meganlynn was waking up.

"You know Meg," he spoke as she was sleeping. "I have always loved you. I think that I always will. You are the one thing in my world that I would say completes me. You encourage me so much.

"You may think that I am a horrible guy, but I'm not. I do love you more than anyone. I want to be the one to hold you, love you. I want to wake every day of the rest of my life and see your face." He was crying.

"Then why didn't you just say that in the first place?" Meganlynn whispered.

"I tried, but I just couldn't get the right words to come out," he answered truthfully.

"What happened to me since the flight?" she asked.

"You're talking," he said, pausing for a minute. "You're talking!" He reached over to her bed and then gave her a hug just as she was sitting up.

"Yeah, you've been carrying on a conversation with me."

"Yeah for like two seconds! But you're awake! You're awake!"

"Yeah." She could barely talk because Blue had kicked her in the throat so hard. "But—what did I break?"

"He broke a couple of ribs and he ripped a couple of muscles so bad that they had to sew them back together."

"How did Blue do it?"

"You didn't let him do anything Meg; you were trying to get away."

"But it was my fault, Justin."

"How was this your fault?"

"Because I was the one who was asking for it, and I let it happen. If I had wanted to stop it then I could have." Meganlynn was trying not to cry.

"That is a lie, Meg. You know that. Was it your fault when he first sexually harassed you?"

"No."

"Were you asking for that?"

"No."

"How in the world were you asking for this?"

"Because it was the second time that this has happened in a year, and it can't possibly be all his fault."

"And why not?"

"Because I'm always wrong! I was asking for it."

"If you are always wrong then you are truly wrong about this. You didn't ask for it."

"Were my parents here?"

"Why wouldn't they be?"

"Because they don't exactly care."

"What did Blue do to you?"

"Everything! He did everything!" she screamed.

"Yeah, I know that. You're going to hurt yourself even more than Blue has already. Your dad can't eat anything here, and they were really hungry."

"I don't know what I'm thinking anymore."

"I know." He sat down at the side of her bed and held her.

"Justin?"

"Yeah?"

"Did you really mean all of those things that you were saying?" her eyes begging for him to say that they were true.

"Why wouldn't I?"

"I don't know."

"You were wondering weren't you?"

"Pretty much."

"Okay."

"Yeah." Justin just assumed that she was getting the doctor after they heard Meganlynn doctor's name was called over the loud speaker.

They waited for a few more minutes. Justin had to tell Meganlynn everything that had gone on during that day. She remembered some of it.

"I love you," he said. That was the first time that Justin had said that to Meganlynn in a long time.

"I love you, too," she said back kind of scared, fearing that he would start laughing at her and reject her just as he had before. She had missed him. She sat up in her bed and thought about everything that had happened on the plane, but she was confused about everything that had happened there.

"How are you now that you have woken up?" the doctor asked Meganlynn as she walked in.

"Good, I think," Meganlynn answered, sounding confused.

"Really? Can you remember enough to tell the police anything right now?"

"I don't think that I can." Meganlynn was trying to remember anything that she could. "Okay." The doctor did not know what to do. "What can you remember about the plane ride?"

"Not much."

"I remember more than she does," Justin told her.

"Okay, but that's not going to help us," the doctor replied.

"Justin, stay here with me please," Meganlynn pleaded.

"I think I know what is going on with you."

"What? Please, someone tell me." Meganlynn had a worried look on her face and looked from the doctor to Justin back and forth. Justin knew what the doctor was saying.

"Does she have that?" he asked the doctor.

"Have what?" Meganlynn asked looking back to Justin.

"I don't think so," the doctor replied.

"Oh," Meganlynn replied, sitting back in her bed.

"She remembers some stuff."

"Yeah," Justin told her. He sat down next to her because he knew that this was going to be hard for her to remember. The doctor, moved closer to the two of them.

"Can I send the cops in?" the doctor asked Meganlynn.

"Yeah." She nodded her head along with the doctor to show that she did understand. Then a small tear inched its way down her cheek and onto the bedspread. The doctor left the room.

"You did really well, Meg," Justin said after she had left the room.

"Really? Because I lied."

"When?"

"When I said that I didn't do anything."

"How did you lie there?"

"Because I said that I didn't do anything. I really probably could've stopped it if I had wanted to. I did provoke it. I deserved it. It was nothing anyway, horseplay really."

"Horseplay got you raped, beaten, and some of your bones broken?"

"I did it when I dressed the way I did. After all, I did wear shorts."

"You were only there for two days, and there isn't any way that Mr. Nolls can put you in marching band."

"Yeah, I know, maybe I can learn a pit part."

"I hope that even if you don't then you can at least do something."

"Yeah."

"Meganlynn, you didn't do anything when he was doing all of his crap to you. You kept your mouth shut, which is all that you are guilty of, and nothing other than that. Now why do you seem to think that you are at fault for everything that he did to you?"

"I know that's probably a pretty stupid thing for me to think."

"I'm going to be honest and say yes, it is a pretty stupid thing for you to think."

"Thanks, I guess, for telling me the truth."

"Anytime you need it." He smiled.

"I know." Then the two police officers came in.

"Hello ma'am. I'm Officer Whimby," he said, pointing to himself. "And this is Officer Dugly," he said, pointing to the other officer standing to his right. "We are here to take your statement."

"Can I ask a question?" Meganlynn asked while they were getting out their pen and paper for the statement.

"Yes, we would love to answer any questions that you have during this."

"Can he be charged for something that I didn't tell the police that tried to take my statement down in Arizona?"

"Yes, you may have to travel to that state so he can be tried in that state and convicted in that state, but other than that, you most certainly can in this case."

"Okay, then I will tell you." Meganlynn did remember every bit of it by this time.

"It all started back in eighth grade. He was sitting in the seat next to me, and he was also in my group for science. He had asked me out a few days before, but I had said no because I had a boyfriend."

"Who was your boyfriend at the time?"

"Justin," she said, pointing to Justin who was sitting right next to her at this point.

"Okay, go on."

"Then, he must have decided that he wasn't good enough for me because then he started to sexually harass me." Meganlynn could not help but sound like she wanted to cry like she actually did.

"What did he say?"

"This is going to take more paper than that."

"Okay, go on anyway."

"During pre-band camp, he was grabbing me and making me kiss him. He was also telling everyone that I was his girlfriend and not Justin's girlfriend.

"Then, on the plane ride to band camp, he made me read him passages from the Bible. I really didn't mind it, but it was just horrifying to have to read them to him and to have sit next him when I really just wanted to sit next to Justin.

"Then, at band camp, he was doing all of the same things. It was the third day when everything started to go all wrong. He then raped me and then beat me so hard that the oldest girl in the cabin went and got my band teacher. By the time that she got back, I was gone because I had ran away to escape it all. My friend had to take me to the hospital because it was so bad.

"The next two days after that, I spent with him. Then he took me to the airport, and we saw that Blue was waiting for me right across where he couldn't go.

"Then on the plane ride home, he and Justin were sitting in front of me. I was in writing and my friend that was sitting next to me had to go to the bathroom. There was then a seat open for anyone to sit in. Then, he went and sat next to me on the plane. My friend came back, and he wouldn't give her back her seat, then I was stuck sitting next to him for the rest of the plane ride home.

"Finally, I had to go to the bathroom. I got up, and went to the bathroom. He then followed me because he knew that I was panicking with him. Then he forced himself into the bathroom with me and then proceeded to rape and beat me. He kicked me in the neck, making my voice really scratchy, and then my legs, hurting them. He also kicked me just about everywhere else on me. Plus, I won't be surprised at all if I can't have kids anymore. Then, I was laying there, and he took my legs and broke both of them so I had to crawl were ever I needed to go. He was going to go and do something, and he left me there to suffer. I was bleeding harder and harder by the second, and then Justin came in and found me. He went and got the pilot, flight attendant, and Mr. Nolls. Then I don't really remember anything else because I was asleep."

"What a story you'll have to tell when your kids are going to school."

"Yeah." Meganlynn was crying by this point. She had stayed strong enough to give the policemen the information that they needed, but other than that, she really had needed to cry about the whole deal.

"Thank you for your statement. Do you have any witnesses?"

"I am," Justin said, standing up. "Who was that guy that you were hanging around all of the time while we were down in Arizona?"

"Johnny." Meganlynn's voice was nearly gone. She had to yell just for Justin to hear her.

"He's one and so are Lizzie, Taylor, and Morgan because they were all there when it happened."

Meganlynn was nodding her head.

"I think that's about it though," Justin answered.

"Thank you. Do you want to press charges?"

Meganlynn nodded her head again. She was not scared in the dream; she was brave and was hopeful enough to stay away from Blue, and to have him do the same to her.

"Meg," she heard a voice say as she was still dreaming. She woke-up and her parents were standing in front of her.

"Mom? Dad?" she asked sleepily.

"Yes, honey?" her mother answered.

"Are you guys back?" she asked as she laid her head down on the pillow that was behind her.

"Yeah, honey, we're right here," her mother answered; she had missed her daughter. She was scared that Meganlynn was never going to wake up. Blue was now going to be tried for beating, rape, and sexual harassment, and there would not be any way that he could escape that. Meganlynn was just a little bit excited about it.

"What time is it?" she asked once she had finally become aware that it was light out

"About seven thirty, sweetheart."

"Oh, I thought that it was still almost eight thirty at night."

"Are you confused?" her father asked.

"Very," she answered. "I really don't know what happened, Daddy."

"What has happened to her after she woke-up?" her father asked as he turned toward Justin.

"A lot."

"Explain, please."

"Okay, she woke up while you were gone. Like, right after you had gone is when she woke up. The police came in and they asked her some hard questions. She was scared, and it was extremely hard for her to talk about, but she somehow got through it."

"Did she press charges?"

"Not down in Arizona, but up here she did."

"She's all right now?"

"Seems to be, but I think she really confused."

"Well, when she seems not to understand any of the things that she normally understood, and now, she just lost her memory because of something that this Blue did. Well, I think that I have a right to be upset."

"I was helping your daughter that night."

"Where were you when all of you were down in Arizona?"

"I was off hanging out with my friends. She was off hanging out with that Johnny kid."

"Johnny was helping her?"

"He was with her ever since the first day of band camp."

"How did he know when she was down there?"

"We went to see him and her aunt and uncle right when we got to Arizona."

"Did he seem like he still loved her?"

"Yeah, they seemed as though they still liked each other, I guess."

"Huh, wonder why Johnny didn't tell us?"

"They probably tried, but I would imagine that they would've had a little bit of a problem getting through."

"Maybe."

"Ask Meganlynn when she wakes-up."

"Yeah, I guess I could." He was curious and wondering why these things were happening to his family all at the same time.

"Look, they probably didn't even think about it. Megan was going through a lot down there. Johnny was probably trying to keep her sane."

"Could anyone keep her sane?"

"No one could. I was horrified to know that the comforter, the person that keeps every one sane at that school, to know that she now needed comforting."

"She keeps everyone sane?"

"She always has every since seventh grade."

"Wow, no wonder she knows a lot about everyone's business."

"Yeah, everyone could call her, day or night."

"And she would listen?"

"Yeah, if we lost her, it would be like the end of the world for the school."

"I can see that, and it wouldn't be the only thing that her dying would be the end of the world for."

"Who else?"

"Our church, our family, all of her and our friends, the pets, and the neighbors."

"Can't forget all of the teachers and English teachers that have taught her."

"Yeah, that too," her father's eyes began to water a little. He could not help but guess at what life would be like without Meganlynn.

⁓

Meganlynn had fallen asleep a few hours earlier. She felt empty, alone, and needy. She wanted someone that would listen to her. She missed herself when she was in seventh grade, but now, it felt as though she could never get that girl back.

The doctor walked in while her parents and Justin were still asleep.

"The good news is that you don't have any STDs, but the bad news is that you may have flashbacks. Things may become even clearer as time goes on, things that you didn't even have anything to with."

"What are the things that are going to become clearer for me?" Meganlynn asked as the doctor was talking to her.

"Mostly things that he did to you."

"Like?"

"The beatings, the raping, and the things that he said to you. Do you have a way of getting all of your feelings out?"

"I can write, which normally takes most of the pain away."

"Right, when you write, but what about after you stop writing?"

"Well, texting my best friend helped when he was sexually harassing me in eighth grade, but my aunt had to stop it because I went over."

"So, writing really did help, but what about talking to someone?"

"Yeah, I will talk to all of my friends, my parents, and anyone else that will listen."

"So, talking, texting, and writing all helped. What happens when no one will listen?"

"I blow up."

"How?"

"I just go all up in flames as I am about to tell someone about whatever is going on."

"Do you shout it out?"

"No, I can't take it anymore."

"What happens then?"

"Then it normally comes out some way or another."

"Well, who did go to the last time?"

"My eighth grade English teacher."

"How did she find out?"

"Because we were doing poetry for one of the English projects. We had to write a poem, and I chose to write one about a person that was doing something to me in my life that was life changing."

"Can you tell me what the poem said?"

"Yeah, I pretty much know it by heart."

"Would you like to tell me, or write it down?"

"Write it down."

"Have a notebook with you?"

"Yeah, there's one in my laptop bag. Actually, I have it saved on my laptop."

"Can you show me?"

"Yeah." Then Meganlynn got her laptop out of the bag.

"Is your computer booted up?"

"Yeah, actually it's right here." She pulled the poem up. "Here." She turned the computer screen toward to the nurse so she could see it.

Blue

Blue
Unforgiving, unwilling,
Mean, defying, evil,
I feel harassed every time I'm around him—
Blue

"Was this everything that he did to you tied up into one little poem?" she asked when she was done.

"Pretty much, yeah," Meganlynn said once she had put the computer screen back down.

"Wow, he had been abusive to you."

"Very abusive, very."

"Why did you put up with it for so long?"

"Because I was scared. I really didn't know what to do."

"How did you not know what to do? I mean didn't they talk about to this in school?"

"Well, I mean I really couldn't tell what was going on between us."

"What do you mean you couldn't tell?"

"I mean that I couldn't see that he was sexually harassing me."

"Wow, I thought that you might have seen it as plain as day."

"No, you can't."

"How did you finally get the word out about this?"

"See the line that says 'I feel harassed every time I'm around him?'"

"Yes, but what about it?"

"My eighth grade English teacher looked at that and asked me if I really did feel that way. When I told her that I did, she told me that she needed to talk to me after class. I told her everything that went on between him and me. Then she told the principle. I got called down there during seventh hour, and then I had to tell him everything that was going on. We called my parents, and then I was free. I got my stuff out of my locker and then I went home. After Monday finally came, Blue wasn't anywhere to be found. I was happy, and then I was called into the office once again. They told me that he was suspended, and then the police officer told that if he ever did anything else to me, then I needed to get one of the teachers or someone else."

"Wow."

"Yeah. I truly needed a boyfriend at that time, and Justin was my boyfriend at the time. I wanted someone to protect me and tell me that he loved me. That is exactly what he did, but all I really wanted was someone to listen and to hold me as if I was a precious gem that could only be handled with the finest touch."

"Were you?"

"Yeah, he held me tighter than anyone ever did."

"Okay, well I have to go. I was just seeing to it that you were okay and healthy."

"Thank you."

"You bet." She walked out of the door.

"Meg," Justin said as she was laying in the bed.

"What?" she asked sleepily.

"Your parents aren't up, but you and I are now."

"Yeah, key word there, now."

"Only because I woke you up." He put his arm around her and pulled her closer to him so they could at least have a little bit of privacy even if her parents were right there.

"Yeah." She let her head fall on his shoulder and held her arms around his waist.

"Are you okay?" he asked after a while.

"Yeah, I'm fine. I'm really happy that you're here right now, though." He then leaned in and kissed her gently on the lips. Justin's arm stayed around Meganlynn, and Meganlynn's arms stayed around Justin's waist.

CHAPTER 10

Meganlynn was scared, but she was now out of the hospital.

"Here," Justin said as he helped her into the car once they were leaving the hospital.

"Thanks," she said as he helped her.

"Yeah." They were able to go back to the house that Meganlynn wanted to be in so bad. She wanted more than anything to be normal again, but she knew that she would never be able to play like a normal teenager for the rest of the marching band season.

"How was marching band?" Meganlynn asked Justin once they had gotten on the road.

"Boring, and we really didn't have a whole lot to do without you there. Everyone was really worried about you the days that you weren't there. Your friends were scared to death. You were the one that kept the whole band normal, and then you were gone."

"Why would anyone really care a whole lot about everything?"

"Because everyone loves you, and they need you to stay sane."

"All I really want right now is to be invisible."

"I know," he said pulling her into his embrace and trying to comfort her the best way that he possibly could.

"What classes do you have?"

"I have every hour with you, besides seventh hour."

"Hello?" Meganlynn's mother answered the phone that was ringing in the front seat. "I understand. Yes. Yes."

Once they were back to her home, they had to get her up to the front door.

"Am I allowed to go to school tomorrow?" Meganlynn asked.

"Yeah, with Justin's help."

"I have all of the same classes as her except seventh hour."

"Why not seventh hour?"

"Because she had creative writing, and then I have engineering."

"Oh," she answered.

"I know people that have the same class though."

"And they would keep her away from Blue?"

"They should."

"Should?"

"If I asked them to, then they probably would."

"Okay, I can deal with that."

"Okay."

"Where did Meganlynn go?" Meganlynn's mother asked when she saw that Meganlynn was gone.

"Probably to her room."

"Probably? Go look." He went down the hallway to her bedroom. They had brought everything back upstairs from the room that she had had downstairs. It would make it easier for Meganlynn to be there in her room when she wanted to be.

"Are you okay, Meg?" Justin asked when he found her.

"I guess." Her voice was still hoarse and frail. She was barely able to talk.

"Hey, come over here." He stepped inside of the room and sat down on her bed. "Are you okay?"

"I'm just so confused at the moment; I honestly don't know what to do."

"Okay, but do you know what you want?"

"I'm trying. I don't even know if I'll ever be able to play softball again."

"Well, if you're not able to, I'm sure that they'll let you at least be their manager if they have one. They know how well you can play."

"Maybe, but softball is the only sport that I ever actually got." Meganlynn sat back on her bed. Justin sat on her bed and rubbed her arm.

"Well, maybe there was a reason that you weren't supposed to play softball for however long you aren't allowed to play softball."

"Yeah, there probably will be, if that."

"I think that you'll be able to be in softball this year. I know that you'll be fine to play softball. I just know."

"Thanks, Justin."

"At least softball season doesn't start next week."

"Yeah, you're right."

"Glad that you can see it my way."

"Yeah." Meganlynn was still not happy.

She had never been able to see it other ways; she just wanted everything to be the same again. She knew that her wish was barely possible and not even going to happen. She was scared and felt alone. Even with Justin sitting right by her on her bed, she still felt as though she was the only person on the face of the earth. No one in her home understood anything she was going through or what she feared. She knew that she would never be the same person that she had once been, but she would have to make the most of her bad experience.

They sat there for a while longer. Justin held Meganlynn around her waist. Her parents had brought her television up from her room in the basement and placed it in her old room. Justin turned it on and began to watch a movie with her. After about an hour and a half, Meganlynn's mother came to the door and told them that it was time for dinner.

They sat in the living room so the whole family could watch the show that was on. Most of the shows that they were watching were funny.

"I'm going to my room," she said, and she walked away from the rest of the family.

"Do you want me to come with you?" Justin asked.

"No, I need some time by myself."

"Okay, I'll be in there in a little while."

"Fine." She went the rest of the way without another word.

"People are going to make fun of her when we get back in school. They are so mean at our school," Justin said as he turned back to Meganlynn's mother and father.

"This is her favorite TV show, and she wants to go in her room," her father said sadly.

"Can she turn it on in her room?"

"She can now because we just hooked it up today. She'll be surprised if she can find out that the TV station will come in."

"We may just hear something come from her room, then."

"Yeah, just maybe."

"When should I go in there?"

"In about ten minutes."

"Okay."

Meganlynn was completely happy sitting in her room alone without anyone to see her, talk to her, or touch her. She was so scared of Blue that nothing even mattered to her anymore. Not her friends, boyfriend, movies, books, family, not even her written work.

What am I willing to do in order to get published? She asked herself, trying to get her mind off of Blue. *Right now, absolutely nothing.* She felt as though nothing in the world could actually bring her to have a smile on her face.

Justin walked down the hallway as he wondered why she was acting the way that she was. He wondered while he walked down the hallway. He opened her door and saw her turning the TV on then sitting down on her bed and writing stuff on the notebook she had in her hands. He did not enter the room for a few seconds as he saw a tear drop from her eyes to the paper that was placed in front of her. He walked in and placed his arm around her shoulders to make her feel as though there was someone there for her no matter what.

"Megan, you're okay. I'm here. Your parents are here. Mostly, everyone you love is here." He shook her but all of the examples just made her cry just hearing them. "Meg, you get to go to the mall tomorrow."

"What, do you just want me to be happy because, oh, I get to go shopping tomorrow?" she screamed at him when he was done. Her face showed the physical and emotional pain and fear that she was going through her eyes.

"No, I was just telling you some good things that are going on in your life."

"Well, guess what! The little Christian girl has finally had a horrible experience! Forgive me for being scared! Forgive me," she took a breath, "for having a horrible experience! Forgive me that I have absolutely no idea how in the world I am going to live through this! Forgive me because Blue wasn't arrested! Forgive me that he chose to do all of this to me! Forgive me for never telling you why he did this even though I have absolutely no idea why he did this to me! I'm sorry that you have no want or desire to hear my issues at this point because you obviously think that can cheer me up from rape, beating, sexual harassment, and stalking! Forgive me for suddenly not being able to want to go shopping tomorrow! Forgive me for being scared! Forgive me for wanting to save my virginity for my future husband! Which, there is no way in Hell that you will ever be him! I'm sorry that you're a jerk for not even caring enough to knock on the door when you came in! I'm sorry that you are the one person that is here instead of Johnny! Especially since you were the one that was there when Blue was raping me the first time! Forgive me for forgiving you! Forgive me for not wanting to write! Forgive me for wanting to be alone! Forgive me for making that so obvious! Forgive me for everything that I did right! Forgive me for trying to do the right thing! Forgive me for trying to do the nice, Christian thing that the Bible tells us to do! I'm sorry that you're such a jerk that you can't even see what in the world is actually going on right now! I'm sorry that my pain is just way too real for you to handle! I'm sorry that you know the walls between us will never fade away! I'm sorry that when I was crying, you were *never there* to wipe away all of my tears! I'm sorry that when I slept that you were *never* there to fight away all of my fears! I'm sorry that the only reason that you know everything that went on is because you were *right there* watching all of it happen! Also sorry on that subject because, that was the only way that you were *ever* going to find out!"

"Why?" he asked taken back by her comments that she had made to him.

"Because you wouldn't have done anything anyway!" She looked over at the door to see her parents standing in the doorway. "and I was also so mad at you for just standing there while Blue was raping me! Who knows other than God for Pete's sake?" Her voice dropped as she realized that her father was standing there. "You were right there. Standing, watching, and helping!" She screamed more at him as time went on.

"How could you possibly know that? You've tried so many things to forget, and Satan is always there, and he probably made you think that it actually happened. He didn't rape you, beat you, sexually harass you, nor did he stalk you," Justin said in a sweet, calming voice. Her parents crossed their arms as they listened to the conversation that they were having. Meganlynn's mother tried to walk in the room, but her husband stopped her from walking in.

"I think I would know what happened that night!" she screamed back at him. "I was there and fully awake and fully able aware of what was happening. Especially since it lasted for over an hour!"

"Shut-up!" he yelled back. Her father tried to take a step forward and her mother stopped him before he got into the room. "You just shut-up and listen for once in your life!"

"No! I am not going to 'shut-up and listen' to one of the people who raped me! I owe nothing to you—no, not even one little ounce of respect!"

"You can't control anything that you want me to forgive you for!"

"I do not need your forgiveness." Her voice then got very cold, deep, quite, and serious.

"Look at you, you're pathetic!"

Her mother walked in the room and stood between the two teens. "That's enough!" her mother shouted at Justin. Justin stepped back away from her mother.

"What do you expect me to do? What do you mean that you don't need my forgiveness? Don't you need it to get to heaven?"

"No, I need to forgive you because it could keep me from Heaven. I don't need you to forgive me at all."

"Then guess what?"

"What?" she asked sarcastically.

"You deserved to lose your virginity."

"No she didn't!" her father shouted as he stepped in front of Justin.

"I guess you would say that."

"Why?" he asked, giving him the death stare.

"Because your daughter is such a bitch that I really don't mind saying it to your face or her face." He turned to see Meganlynn. "The truth hurts, huh?"

"No, not for me."

"Why not?"

"Because that's not the truth."

"No, it's not!"

"No, I forgot that I help anyone whenever I possibly can. I forgot that I absolutely am nice to anyone when I can be. I didn't tell on Blue for a month because I was giving him chances to stop doing his crap! I can honestly say that I forgot that I will talk to anyone even when they absolutely hate me. I'm sorry that I forgot that I'm conceded, and it's not my fault. Do you see where I'm going?"

"No."

"Well, why don't you just try to understand? I know that you have the brain the size of a peanut, but you can concentrate on something long enough, then maybe you'll actually understand it."

"You slut!" he shouted as he walked near the door.

"Please just let me go," Meganlynn pleaded as she watched him walk out the door of her room.

"If I do, and it is out of anger, then I will lie on the witness stand."

"Go right ahead, they can then get you on that also!"

"They may be able to, but it would so be worth it!"

"Hope you have a fun time in Hell then."

"Oh trust me, I will."

"Why? Because you can then rape any girl that you possibly want to?"

"Yeah, and I'm sure that Blue would be even happier in there because he could actually keep someone safe in there."

"Just like you could keep me safe?"

"Yeah, and trust me I could."

"But you won't."

"Yeah."

"How am I in less need of protection than I was last year?"

"Because last year you dealt with the sexual harassment that you asked for, and this year you got everything else that you deserved."

"No, I didn't ask for any of this to happen."

"Well, we also know that you deserved all of the things that you got."

"No, she didn't," Meganlynn's mother said as she walked over to the door. "No one deserves to be raped. Not if you're a murderer and not if you're a Christian girl."

"Fine, I'm sorry."

"Thank you," Meganlynn's father said to Justin. "Now, apologize to Meganlynn."

"I'm sorry."

"Thank you, but you need to apologize to Meganlynn," her mother said to him.

"I am very sorry for hurting you Meganlynn."

"You're sorry for what?" Meganlynn asked him.

"I'm sorry for just standing there while Blue was doing all of the horrible things to you."

"And what else?"

"There's more?"

"How about all of the things that you just said to her?" her mother asked.

"Okay, I'm sorry for all of those things that I said also."

"I forgive you."

"You what?"

"I forgive you for saying all of the mean and horrible things earlier, but you just stood there while Blue did everything to me. You'll have to understand that I just can't get over that in a second. You were there, and you didn't even have the common courtesy to try to get him off of me or to try and get someone that could've helped. I can't get over that."

"I don't know how you can't forgive me for that."

"You were standing right there watching him do everything to me."

"You were right there also."

"No dip! I was the one who was being raped."

"Well, you still could've gone and got someone."

"Even though that may be the case, I don't care. I was the one who was scared to get out of the car with my nice and loving boyfriend. I knew that he couldn't even go past the gate because he wasn't a member of the band. We knew that Blue was going to do something to me right after he left. Unfortunately, it was right after I walked through the gate whether he was gone or not."

"But still—"

"But still what? What could I have possibly done?"

"You're right, you were the innocent one. You were the one that wasn't at fault. You were the one that was hurt the worst."

"I was! I am that person that you just described!"

"Yeah, I was the one who was hurt the worst."

"Not unless you were killed by Blue, which you wouldn't even be here if that was the case then you would probably have a worse experience, only yours would be for an eternity because you would be in Hell."

"How do you know that?"

"Because you were standing right there watching, and I highly doubt that you would ever even ask God for forgiveness. The only reason that you were acting like you were saved was to get in my pants."

"Why don't you just shut-up, you lost your virginity to Blue."

"Not willingly."

"It doesn't matter. God will probably send you to Hell for giving it away."

"He is a caring God. He is a loving God. He is a forgiving God. He will love me no matter what because He is a loving God. He will absolutely love me even though this was 'my fault' or at least it was to you."

"Yeah right, I'm as much of a Christian as you are."

"I am a Christian."

"You don't act it."

"Yeah right."

"Is that why you won't sit on my lap?"

"One of the reasons, the other is because I just don't feel like sitting on someone's lap that I know is not going to be my husband for the rest of my life."

"When we get old enough, you and I are getting married."

"Yeah," she answered sarcastically.

"Hah, you'll never make it to Heaven. I should be your husband."

"Oh, and why?"

"Because I am the best guy that you could ever get."

"And I'm supposed to believe this why?"

"Because you're stupid. You're a blonde. You're a woman."

"Excuse me?"

"You're a woman; you're supposed to be stupid."

"You try being a woman, you'll find out how incredibly smart we are."

"Yeah right."

"Just get out."

"Why?"

"Because I'm too stupid to sleep anyway."

"Exactly."

"Should I be nervous?" she asked, cornering Justin out of the door.

"Why?" He backed to where he was finally out of the doorway.

"I can't remember how to breathe." She shut the door in his face and went over to her desk.

Justin looked at the door. He was mad, angry, and upset. She was horrified that she was acting like this. Meganlynn had never acted as though she actually had a brain. He touched her doorknob and turned it.

"What?" Meganlynn asked as she was typing on her computer. Justin shut the door behind him very quietly.

"Why would you say that you and Justin would never get married?" Justin asked in a voice that he tried to make sound like her mother's.

"Because he's disgusting, and he's just like Blue," she answered.

"He's not disgusting." She turned around to find Justin standing behind her.

"What do you want and why is my door closed?"

"I want you, and because we are actually going to do something other than kiss." His hands reached out and grabbed her. He threw her on to her bed. "With your two broken legs this is going to be quite the issue."

"What is?" Meganlynn asked as she sat up straight on the bed.

"Sex."

"You know that I would never ever even think about doing anything like this with anyone but my husband."

"Maybe, but I am your future husband."

"No you're not."

"Yes I am."

"There is no way in—" He hit her.

"I am going to be your future husband and we are going to have sex tonight."

Meganlynn woke-up with her pants off of her legs and Justin gone. She wanted to know what had happened.

Did he really rape me? She thought to herself as she grabbed the clothes that were laying on the ground. *I don't have any clothes on and I'm all jittery. He did. He had to. Great, I've been raped again. I'm calling Johnny, I have to. Wait, Johnny may have e-mail. I'll get on and see if he does.* Meganlynn picked up one of her pillows to sit on in the chair and noticed a note left by Justin.

My love, she read. *I love you with all of my heart. Even though I wasn't the one that got your virginity, I know that you would've given it to me anyway. I love you with all of my heart. I am also going to say that if you ever don't get married to me when I ask, then I am going to do the same thing that I told you I would do if you yelled for your parents. I will kill your family and make you watch them all die a slow and painful death. Then I will lock you in a room with a lot of pictures of your relatives that died for the rest of your life. I will keep you alive until your heart finally gives out, and then you can go to your 'God,' and I will probably be in hell just as you have said, but I will never leave you alone. You should know that with how obsessed I am with you. I really do love you more than anything. Get over Blue; he was just as obsessed with you as I am. You and I will be together one day and by the way, you are no longer allowed to wear white with a clear conscience. I love you, and you were so much fun last night. Love, Justin.*

Enjoy Justin. She sat there in the quietness of her bedroom. Then, she pulled on her clothes. She was hard at work on her book when her parents walked in.

"Are you ready, sweetheart?" her mother asked her.

"Yeah, I guess."

"Okay, are you feeling better today?"

"Not really. Is Justin going with us?"

"No, but I have someone better that is coming with us today."

"Who?"

"Well, let's just say that you miss him a lot."

"Okay. How much longer until we pick him up?"

"He's staying in Detroit, so about three hours."

"Okay, should I take my notebook or something to do?"

"Yes, we are going to the Cincinnati Mall, so yes you should."

"Okay, I'll grab my stuff and then I'll be right out."

"Okay, we'll be right out there."

"Okay." Meganlynn started to get her stuff around. Her mother sat down on her bed.

"What happened yesterday when Justin shut your door?"

"He threatened and raped me."

"What?"

"He did the same thing that Blue did, only minus the sexual harassment, and beating, and plus the threatening that if I didn't marry him then he would, well, it says on here," she handed her mother the note with the details on it. Her mother read it, and looked up at her daughter, surprised when she was done.

"Meganlynn, why didn't you yell or something?"

"He would've done what he said in that note."

"There is no way that you are going marry him."

"I know."

"Does he believe this?"

"Yeah, but if I show the judge and lawyer that, there is no way that he will ever see the light of day again."

"Isn't that the necklace that he got you?" she pointed to the cross that was around her neck.

"Yeah," Meganlynn said as she looked down at it.

"What does it say again?"

"It says: *The Lord is my Sheppard. Ye, though I walk through the valley of darkness, I shall fear no evil for the* LORD *is my Sheppard.*"

"He knew you pretty well, didn't he?"

"Yeah, he knows me very well."

"Let's go shopping, honey, that'll get your mind off of this."

"Yeah, let's go and get whomever we're going to get now."

"Got everything?"

"Yeah." They left the house.

They picked up Johnny to take him with them. They went shopping for the rest of the day and took Meganlynn back home. Johnny was now living back in Michigan, where he was needed most of all. He was there to protect

Meganlynn and to keep her safe while she was in school. He was now her boyfriend. Johnny and Meganlynn were sitting in her room, watching a movie when Justin called.

"Should I answer it?" she asked him. Johnny knew the things that had gone on between her and Justin.

"Yeah, I'll pause the movie," Johnny said as he paused the movie. Meganlynn answered the phone.

"Hello?" she asked as she put it on speaker phone so Johnny could hear it.

"Hey, Meg, or should I say, baby?"

"I am not your baby."

"Yeah right, you read the note."

"Yes, and I would like to thank you for that evidence."

"Whatever, fact is that I raped you and now that two guys have done you, there is nothing you can do other than be called a total slut." Johnny took the phone out of Meganlynn's hands and then set it down on her bed.

"And why should I be at fault for you raping me?" Johnny and Meganlynn were sitting in front of her parents having them listen to the conversation. Meganlynn's mother got the voice recorder and started recording.

"Because you're a slut for letting two guys do you."

"I never let two guys do me. Two guys have raped me, but never have they ever had my consent."

"Whatever, slut."

"Hang-up the phone," Johnny told her as they sat in the living room.

"I am not a slut!" she screamed, and then she hung-up the phone. Her parents looked at her, and then she decided to go back on her room. Johnny left to go with her. Johnny did not really make a big deal out of it. He was not going to talk until she talked. He figured that it was the best way to get her to talk to him. She thought it was too.

"He sat there and watched it happen."

"Who, Meg? Who sat there and watched?"

"Justin, he just sat there and watched it all happen."

"Well, Justin is a moron."

"You're right."

The first day of school had finally come, three weeks later. Blue and Justin were still in band and in school. Johnny joined band, and then made Meganlynn feel safer than she did before. Johnny had every class with her. If Blue did not have the class with her, then Justin did. The good thing was that Johnny had his arms around her or had his hand in her hand whenever he could.

"So, I guess this means that you and I are done?" Justin asked as he walked up to Meganlynn.

"Yeah, we were done when you raped me."

"Yeah, when fire can suddenly freeze is when I raped you."

"Trust me, God can do it."

"Whatever, just remember what's going to happen now. Dark room, all those pictures, dead relatives."

"Back off."

"Who are you?"

"Johnny."

"Big deal, you couldn't protect her if her life depended on it."

"I'd do a better job than you would ever do."

"Yeah right, you wouldn't protect that little slut for nothing."

"Yes I would."

"No one else would, why should you?"

"Because, unlike you, I actually know how a real man acts."

"Yeah right. Meganlynn, he's just trying to get in your pants."

"No he's not. He's a Christian; he can at least do a little bit of a better job of controlling himself."

"Good luck, slut."

"Yeah look at you, slut," Blue said, walking up behind her and slapping her butt.

"Get your hands off of her," Johnny said, jerking his head around.

"What are you going to do about it?" Blue asked.

"Just, please, keep your hands off her."

"What? You actually like the whore as much as we do?"

"I know that you guys are like—obsessed with her, but you need to get over it because you both never get her. I know that, she knows that, all of her friends know that, everyone knows that, and I'm pretty sure that both of you know that."

"Whatever, just know that there will be all of those pictures, and there will always be Blue and me," Justin said as they walked away.

"Johnny. Don't let them hurt me, please," Meganlynn said as she hugged him. He held her close.

"I won't, Megan, I won't."

CHAPTER 11

Every time that Johnny was gone because he was at the office or somewhere else, Meganlynn was raped by both Blue and Justin.

"Are you going to prom, Meganlynn?" Justin asked her.

"Yes," she said.

"Will you go with me?" he asked. Blue stood behind her.

"What are you doing, asking her to the prom? I thought that we agreed that I was going to take her to the prom if any one of us took her," Blue said as he walked over to Justin and Meganlynn.

"Well, what if she turns you down?"

"How come you went back on your promise?"

"Why are you questioning me like this?"

"Because you said that you wouldn't take her to the prom. We agreed that I would be the one taking her to the prom. We also agreed that if I couldn't take her then no one could."

"I remember that." Justin and Blue came toward her in a very strange way, almost horrifying.

"What are you doing?" she asked, backing away. The door was very close to her by now.

"We would like to take you to prom Meganlynn."

"Stop," she said, looking back.

"No, I don't think that we're going to."

"Please, let me have one night to myself."

"No, we're greedy."

"Then have a little, tiny bit of a heart instead of a whole big part of a black hole."

"Never."

"It's just like you to say that."

"I know, right?"

"Now, please, get away from me." She ran out the door and down the hallway. Her fourth hour was advanced placement English Literature, and she made a run for the door that was suddenly so far away.

"Never! Meganlynn, get back here!" They shouted, running after her. The bell rung and the halls started to crowd after about half a second. Johnny was nowhere to be seen.

Meganlynn frantically looked around the halls. Johnny was gone.

"Meganlynn!" Johnny called. She knew that Justin and Blue were still chasing her. Meganlynn ran over to Johnny.

"What do you want with her?" Johnny asked Justin and Blue when they had gotten to where she was standing.

"We were just asking her to prom," Justin stupidly answered.

"Yeah, sure, there's about as much truth there as there is in the world of divination."

"Well, you know there could be some truth there."

"Get away from her. Stay away from her. If I catch you around her again, then you can kiss your lives good-bye."

"We'll chop her up into little tiny pieces."

"If you can ever get near her again."

"We've been a lot nearer to her than you ever will be."

"Did they rape you again, Meg?" Johnny asked turning toward her. She nodded her head. "You ever rape her again, and the cops won't even be able to get their hands on you."

"Why don't we just take her right here and right now instead of taking her at the prom?"

"Yeah, I'll hold him, and you take her. You're a lot better at threatening than I am anyway." Justin took a swing at Johnny, but all Johnny did was hold Meganlynn even tighter than ever. Johnny held her in hope that someone would tell someone.

"Come on Meganlynn!" Blue yelled, grabbing her by her hands and then dragging her off toward the door.

"What?" Justin hit Johnny right in the right cheek. After Johnny was laying down on the ground, Justin ran off to follow Meganlynn and Blue.

"Did you get her?" he asked as he caught up with them out of breath.

"No, we're just running away very, very fast for absolutely no reason."

"You never know."

"Just get in the driver's seat and drive away."

"Where to?"

"Let's go to Detroit. No one will find us there, and Meganlynn can make it back in time for the prom this weekend."

"What are we going to do for a dress for her?"

"That's what plastic's for." Blue held up a shiny plastic credit card that looked like it was brand new and had never been used.

That didn't make you sound like a girl or a shopaholic at all, Meganlynn thought to herself.

"Oh, well after prom, what are we going to do?" Johnny asked pathetically.

"We're going to disappear. We're going to make it look as though Johnny killed a fake Meganlynn, that'll take care of him. Then we can go and do as we please. One of us will marry her, and the other will have an affair with her. I think that I will marry her because I did see her first and have known her for the longest between us."

"Fine, you're right, I guess."

"Just drive."

Jerks, you think that I'm a piece of property. I'm actually a person that has a mind and feelings. I wish that they could see that, but I am the one that should know that will never happen. I am never going to be gone from here, am I? she thought to herself as they drove toward Detroit.

The drive seemed to take forever. She was trying to figure out a way to get out. They stopped at a gas station soon after they had been in the car and had gotten out of Jackson County.

"Would you like a drink?" Justin asked as he got out of the car.

"Just a cola, please," Meganlynn answered.

"Okay, and you, Blue?"

"Same," he turned back to Meganlynn. "Now look, when we get to Detroit, you can buy anything that you want. I have a laptop and everything. You cannot buy a cell phone or anything with a internet connection or any other way to get into connection with the outside world. You need a dress and shoes and accessories. You need more than anything. You will need clothes of any sort. Dancing shoes, high heels and other types of shoes that you want or need. You need everything. But do not buy anything other than that."

"Can I buy a laptop to write on?"

"Sure, you can even get videogames."

"But no internet?"

"Right." Meganlynn looked out the window. She knew everything that she was going buy right then and there. She was going to need high-heeled shoes, shirt, tank tops, and lots of sweatshirts, socks, underwear, bras, laptop, and all of the accessories for whatever else she wanted. And she was going to find the most expensive stores as possible.

When Meganlynn finally woke, she was sitting in the parking lot of the Detroit Mall. She got out and walked in. She walked right down to the nearest electronics store and bought the biggest mp3 player that she could possibly find. She knew that Blue would let her buy whatever movies, audio books, songs and whatever else she could find on it. She bought everything else that she would possibly need. Then, she left and found Blue and Justin once she was done. With about twenty huge bags of things in her hands, they then went down to the nearest restaurant. After they had eaten, she went back to the car and found a place to stay for two nights.

The suite had three rooms in it. One for Justin, one for Blue, and one for Meganlynn. She looked over her room and saw that she did not have a telephone or anything like that. She needed a key to get in and out of the room, which meant that she could not get out of the room without one of the guys. She guessed that they would also lock her room so she would be in there until they let her out. She really did not care; all she wanted was to type. She plugged in the mp3 player to the computer and put all of her music on it.

"I guess that I better put all of my suitcases on here," she noticed that Blue had placed them under her bed. Then she went into the bathroom and put all of her celebrity-style cosmetics away. Then she looked at what else was in her in her bags. She put all of her books on the bookshelves.

She had bought hangers for all of the shirts and pants that she had bought. She hung-up the black and white corset tops. Her grey, white, and purple one-shoulder tops were hung in a straight line. She bought a white, belted, rose-print top; a grey, white, and black spaghetti-strap shirt; another one-shoulder top; and a black top with an empire waist. The normal, plain long-sleeved shirts that she bought were grey, white, light pink, and white. Then she bought five v-neck short-sleeve tops that were black, grey, purple, white, and jade. There were five solid basic tank tops that were white, grey, black, jade, and purple. Then there were the lace-trim tank-tops. There were eleven of these in black, grey, white, purple, red, tan, khaki, blue, denim, coral, and dark grey. She bought several different kinds of long-sleeve shirts with different designs including roses, feathers, butterflies, and other kinds of different things. After all of her shirts were hung-up, she looked through the bags to find where the one that was loaded with her pants from the same store was.

She hung five pairs of velvety sweat pants in the colors of pink, blue, black, purple, and dark blue. Then, she hung her different plaid skirts. Meganlynn honestly hated skirts with all of her might, but Blue had made her buy them, and she was not exactly thrilled about it either.

The shoes were next. They all were heels because that's what Blue had wanted her to wear. Twelve different kinds of boots went into her closet, all neat and clean. Twelve different kinds of dressy shoes went into the closet along with her boots. Then the rest of the shoes were heels that were all over one and a half inches high. Then, she went over to the other bags and got all of other things out. She had never hung so many things that she had needed before. She figured that Blue and Justin had either placed the room under her name or under someone else's name. She was sitting on her bed then she finally, got up, got into sweatpants, and then got into bed and fell asleep.

"Meganlynn! Wake-up! Breakfast!" apparently it was morning. She was being yelled at by Blue and Justin to get out of bed.

"What?" she asked once she got up and went into the bathroom to get ready.

"Breakfast!" yelled Blue.

"Okay, well, I'm not hungry."

"I don't care, get out here and eat!"

"Fine, I'll be out in about five minutes."

"Okay! Be as quick as you can!"

"Yeah!" Meganlynn got her hair brushed and her clothing on. She put on jeans, along with four other shirts underneath a sweatshirt.

Meganlynn went out of her room and into the kitchen. When she looked around, she saw that the room was painted dark and the curtains were shut. All of the normal furniture was gone and all of the happiness, that is if there was any to begin with, was gone from everything. She saw a dress in the corner of the room.

It was a dark purple dress that was floor length. It had ruffles on it and looked as though it feathered out like a bird when it was in pain or shock. The dress had spaghetti straps on it and would make anyone look as though she was a total gothic person.

"Meganlynn," said a deep, dark, voice. "Put on the dress," Meganlynn picked up the dress and started back to her room. "No, Meganlynn, there is plenty of room. Dress out here, please."

If I would've known this was going to happen, I would never have gotten out of bed, Meganlynn thought as she slipped the dress on.

"You will be happy here," Blue said. "Just keep quiet."

How in the world am I supposed to be happy here? she thought as she could make out his figure walking away.

"Now, you are going to marry me at the end of this ceremony."

Oh, you two are definitely going to Hell if you don't get saved! She thought as he told her this.

"Let the ceremony begin!" he yelled.

Can't they hear you downstairs? And what in the world is that supposed to mean that I will 'fall in-love with you and then marry you?' There is absolutely no way ever that I would want to marry you. If Johnny was here, then that would be a different story. I don't want to marry anyone in this room. Blue started to chain her down to the table. *Get off of me!*

"Okay! She is in her wedding dress and there is love in the air." A shadowy figure moved in the corner of Meganlynn's sight. She could not see anything but the figure moving forward.

What kind of love is in the air? Meganlynn wondered.

"Sir, Mr. Priest, please don't wait, she just loves me more than she has ever loved anyone. Please, we are very ready for this," begged Blue.

"Sir, I can honestly say that many things have crossed my path, and I have seen many people love one another as much as you two love each other. This will not be anything different from a normal wedding, I suppose."

"Very well. You must keep her close to you. This being that you treat her really well. She still has her brain, she has just forgotten everything about her old love that she knew. Now, let her be here, and I will make you two married forever and all eternity." Meganlynn suddenly noticed a streak of lightning and a loud boom of thunder.

Lord, help me. I don't want to marry him. I don't want to marry anyone in here. Well, unless Johnny is in this room with me, in which case, he'd better be saving me! she thought to herself.

The priest performed the wedding ceremony. Meganlynn tried to object but when that part came around, Blue just asked him to skip right to the "I do's." Meganlynn was crushed because she had hope at one time that she was finally going to get away from him. She had another chance. She said no when he asked her if she wanted to marry him, and the priest ignored her. He went with Blue's answer no matter what she said.

"Do you feel any different?" Blue asked Meganlynn once the wedding was finally over.

What in the world am I supposed to say? Yes? Why, yes, I feel totally and completely different! Yeah right. She thought to herself, not knowing what to say. *To keep alive, well, and at least partially living, I better agree with him.*

"Yes, I do. I love you," Meganlynn answered with a sweet and faithful voice. *Yeah, I love you, as much as that love potion really worked.*

Wow, I guess a person of the world cannot compare to the power of the Lord. Please, Lord, protect me from these evil people. I think that Satan would truly bless them here on Earth, but down in Hell I think that he is going to condemn them harder than any of his other servants due to the fact that they tried to force the religion on me, but yet, they still couldn't because I was too strong of a Christian. Yeah, there will be some controversy there! Help me, please, Lord, I need to get out of here. I need to be back on the real world to be able to keep my soul and my religion here in the world. I know that other people will keep the Christian religion alive, but still, I would like to go home or at least to the prom before I die. I would like to tell Johnny that I love him and tell my parents and everyone else that I love them also. Please, Lord, let me get out of this situation! I hope you burn forever," Meganlynn told him.

"Yes, well, God does not exist, otherwise you wouldn't be here," Justin said.

"God does exist, and I won't be here much longer."

"How do you know this? You're just a girl."

"I may be 'just a girl,' but I am a very smart girl at that. The only stupid thing that I did was date you."

"Shut up! You little blonde, you don't know anything that is good for you, including me."

"Yeah, you were totally the best thing that ever happened to me," she answered back sarcastically.

"I know I was."

"No, the best thing that ever happened to me is either up in Heaven sitting on His throne, or back at my house with my family waiting for something with me to happen because He truly loves me."

"Who are the two best things that ever happened to you?" Blue asked once he had heard the conversation between Justin and Meganlynn.

"God for one, and Johnny for two."

"Yeah right. Johnny's probably at your house freaking out because he can't find a date for prom. You are just under the impression that he wants to go with you."

"You're a jerk."

"And you just figured this out?"

"No, I'm just now saying it."

"Why didn't that work?" Blue yelled once Justin had began walking back toward him.

"You should have told me that she already found her true love. I can't do the spell if she already has found him, but I can cast a spell on her to become more like you so then her true love will fall out of love with her."

"Do you have any spells that would turn her ugly for the prom?"

"Ugly as in all of the way?"

"No, ugly as in figure."

"Yes, I do. She will turn back from the old hag form at midnight."

"Okay, so we'll just have to leave the prom before then."

"If she doesn't see her actual love, she will believe that he doesn't love her anymore and that he isn't worth it any more. Be there for her, and she will forcefully fall in love with you."

"Sounds good. Now, Meganlynn, you must lie back down on the table."

"I'd rather die."

"Maybe, but you still need to lie down." Justin pushed her back down onto the stone table. She fell onto it as though she had just died all of the suspense.

"Okay, let's get this one on the road. Take her from light. Take her to darkness. She is no longer pretty, but now is ugly!" She was seen as ugly to the men that were in the room, but to the other people that were in the world, she was even more beautiful than ever before.

"Okay, the prom awaits us, Ms. Ugly Betty. Go pack your things we will be leaving after the prom."

"Okay." She went and packed her things silently.

Johnny got his things around for the next day of school. After he was done, he set out in search of GPS that had been set for Meganlynn's phone alone. He had never really been in a situation like this before. He knew that the prom was only hours away by now, but he had every intention of finding her. He wanted to find her with every ounce of energy that he had in him. He looked far and wide all night long. He figured that she had to be somewhere in the city, but he had no such luck in finding her. Then, he went back home for rest and sleep before the big day tomorrow.

"Prom is here!" Justin shouted once Meganlynn had gotten up.

"And your point is?"

"Get into your dress, we're going to get ready for the prom."

"Oh! So exciting!" she yelled sarcastically. She got up and got the long, blue dress on. Her dress was floor length. The top fit perfectly to her form with fake diamonds and pearls around the top and then glistening back down once again. Then, the skirt flailed out giving the perfect image of a total princess. It curved around her on the floor just as a wedding dress would. The top of the dress was covered in sparkles that glistened in the light. Then the top was also lined with glistening fake diamonds and pearls at the top. The skirt was also covered in sparkles, and the bottom was also lined with fake diamonds and pearls.

"Were you being nominated for prom queen, Meganlynn?" Blue asked her as they were walking out the door of the hotel room with the packages of things.

"Actually, yes, I was going to be prom queen."

"Good for you, I guess, but you are not going to be prom queen with those ugly looks."

"Maybe looks don't matter to them, and they will just choose the nicest person that they know, which is still me."

"Still, they won't be able to stand to look at you, let alone vote for you for prom queen."

"I don't care anymore; I just want to see Johnny and the rest of my friends one last time so I can say good-bye to them."

"Your friends, you may say good-be to, but not Johnny. He is way too dangerous."

"For you he is, but for me, he is my knight in shining armor."

"Yeah? Well hopefully you won't be able to see him ever again."

"What if I do?"

"Dark room, no one will be around to hear you scream nor will they be able to rescue you."

"Fine, have it your own way."

"I will. You're such a dumb blonde."

"I'll miss you so much once you're in Hell."

"I hope you do because you are turning your back on the best thing that will ever happen to you."

"Either way, I don't care. There is no—"

"Oh just shut up. I really don't care what in the world that you believe in as a matter of fact."

"Fine," they were in the car and into the salon. *Fine, don't believe; see where it gets you.*

⁓

Her hair was finally done, and it was time for them to start heading for the prom. Thankfully, Meganlynn knew where the prom was being held, or they never would have gotten there. It took them at least three hours before they actually got there. Meganlynn was very excited once they were there. Blue and Justin helped her out of the car.

"Thank you," she said as she grabbed her handbag out of the back seat.

"You're welcome," Blue answered back, holding out his arm for her to hold onto. Meganlynn did not even notice what he was doing, she just walked away so she could get into the prom sooner. She walked up to the entrance and walked in. Blue and Justin followed somewhat closely behind her.

As soon as Meganlynn stepped through the door into the prom, she walked as far away from the door and into the lights that she possibly could. She was hoping that if she could stay in the lights, then maybe she would be able to lose Justin and Blue quicker.

She looked around frantically, she had no idea where she was or where she was going to end up. The girls were all in ball gowns, and the guys were all tuxes that matched their date's dresses. Girls and guys were holding each other close on the dance floor while some guys were there, standing around like wallflowers. Meganlynn looked toward the entrance from the dance floor and saw

Blue and Justin just coming in. She needed to find Johnny more than ever now, she really did not have a choice. She looked through the crowd to see if she could at least see Johnny.

Will he even notice me now since I'm so ugly? Wonder where the bathroom is? Well, if worse comes to worst I can always wait until one of my friends comes in here and tell them to get Johnny to come in here. I wonder if that will work? she thought as she walked around the room. Meganlynn went throughout the room again trying to find Johnny.

Johnny finally got to the prom in just enough time to see Meganlynn going from the car into the prom itself. He followed her in. As she walked around the floor, he followed her trying to get her farther and farther away from the people. Finally, she went into the girls' bathroom. Must be she was trying to fix her makeup, or she was trying to get away from Justin and Blue. His hunch was on the second reason. He followed her in. He knew that he was not allowed in the girls' bathroom, but he really did not have another way to get her out of the bathroom.

He walked in, and he looked for her. She finally caught his eye when he saw her waiting for the bathroom to empty. He saw that she was even more beautiful than he could remember. It seemed as though she glowed with beauty.

"Meganlynn?" he asked walking up behind her.

"Yes?" she asked. He could tell from her voice alone that she was crying.

"Do you even know who I am?"

"Not just by your voice." There was a silence that no one was there to break for Meganlynn and Johnny. "If you're Justin or Blue, I have another hour and a half before I even have to think about the two of you so just go away."

"I would hope that I am not anything like Justin or Blue. I would hope that I traveled a long way for a good reason."

"Where did you come from, because if you see me then you will realize that your long trip to see me was never even worth the time of day."

"Maybe not, but I still traveled all the way from Arizona to see you."

"Still." She stepped out from behind the wall. Johnny's jaw dropped from his mouth enough that she could see. "I must look hideous to you; I wish that I didn't." Her voice was cold and lonely.

"You don't, why do you keep on thinking that you do?"

"Because they had that warlock cast a spell on me."

"Okay, do I have to smack the Christian back into you?"

"No. I don't know what's come over me, Johnny, I just believe it, I guess."

"Stop, or else, I will smack the Christian back into you."

"Yeah, I guess you would."

"It's good to see you again."

"You too. Just wish I was prettier than this."

"Then let the Lord have you see what I see." They walked over to the mirror and stood in front of it.

"What am I looking at?"

"What do you see?"

"I see a beautiful girl in the mirror."

"That's what I see."

"Really?"

"Really. Now let's get you over somewhere besides here. You deserve to be somewhere other than the bathroom on the night that you're about to be named prom queen."

"Fine, let's go back out there, but you can't leave my side. You have to protect me. You have to stand by me, or else, Blue and Justin will take me."

"Yes. Now let's go out there."

"Okay." They went back to the party. Once they got back to the party, they were getting ready to announce the prom queen and prom king.

"And the prom queen is," the announcer said as she stood in front of the microphone. "Is, Meganlynn VanDeritie!" The whole room clapped for her as Johnny walked her up to the stage. He could not let her out of his sight. "The prom king is...Justin Morgan!" They placed the crowns on top of Justin's and Meganlynn's heads. The prom king and queen were not expected to dance with one another, but they were expected to like each other in at least a friendly way. Meganlynn ran down to Johnny, and then, they left.

Blue and Justin were right behind them, trying everything in order to catch them. The only person that they really wanted was Meganlynn. They could not care less about Johnny. For all they knew, that was the person that they were supposed to kill. The pieces were all falling into place. Johnny and Meganlynn both knew that they needed the police station and that was all. After they found that, then Meganlynn would be safe and nothing else would be needed. The police would provide protection and Johnny could be with her no matter what.

"Where's the police station?" Meganlynn breathed as they ran from the prom sight.

"Just down the road from here," Johnny answered, keeping an eye out for Justin and Blue. He knew that they were following. He heard their car engine coming up from behind them. "Over there, in those bushes! Hurry!" Meganlynn dove into the bush, and Johnny dove in right on top of her.

"What happened?" Meganlynn asked, taking her shoes off. There was not any reason for her to make more noise than she should, and her feet were hurting her from all of the running that she had just done.

"Blue and Justin are right behind us, shh." Meganlynn and Johnny were then in complete silence. Meganlynn was panicking from being in the bushes, just praying that Blue would not find her and take her again.

Slowly, but carefully, Justin and Blue walked past them. They kept very quiet and Johnny picked up one of the high heeled shoes that Meganlynn had just taken off. They walked past the two of them not even thinking about where they were going.

Meganlynn and Johnny started back down the street for the police station. They turned the block and Meganlynn was grabbed and pulled almost out of sight.

"Ah!" she screamed as Justin and Blue pulled her waist further and further toward them.

"No!" Johnny yelled back, looking to see that Blue and Justin had taken her back the same way that they had just come from. Meganlynn finally broke free from their grasps.

"Johnny, run!" she screamed as she was running back toward the way that the police station was.

"Megan!" he yelled, grabbing her hand and running back the other way as did Meganlynn.

Finally, the police station was in sight. Meganlynn and Johnny were about to walk up to the stairs when Blue and Justin stepped out in front of them.

He grabbed the high heeled shoe from his pocket that he had been carrying from the bushes and held it in his hands.

"What in the world can you possibly do with a high heeled shoe?" Blue laughed.

"A lot more than you ever will." Meganlynn was behind Johnny's back in order to keep her from danger.

Meganlynn and Justin slipped past them and ran for the front desk.

"Yes?" she asked as she saw that Meganlynn and Justin were in a huge hurry.

"I have found a missing person and there is a terrible threat placed on her life."

"That may be, but still you're still going to have to see the sergeant about a matter this important. Now, you can see Officer Whimby later. Um…does eight-thirty sound okay for you?"

"No, right now sounds okay for us. She's in the missing persons reporting office. Her parents need to be notified that she has been found."

"Oh, well then why did you say that this was an important matter?"

"Because it is." Meganlynn then turned around to see Blue and Justin walking through the double doors that the police station had.

"Um, Johnny," she said quietly.

"What?" he asked her, looking down at her.

"Look." She pointed at Justin and Blue who were now at least fifty feet away from her by now.

"We really need to talk to someone, I do not care if it is the police chief or a sergeant; I don't even care if it is the lowest person on the system as long as they can do something about a raping, beating, attempted murder, and whatever else he did to her, we need to speak to them."

"Sir, I'm sorry, but everyone else is out looking for someone who has been missing for several days, and they actually know who took her. Now, if your friend here is part of missing persons, then I suggest going down there yourself. Now, I am supposed to ask everyone this question: Have you seen this girl?" she asked as she held up a picture of the girl noted to be Meganlynn VanDeritie. Johnny was very angry.

"Why—"

"No, we haven't, sorry for the interruption. Someone thought they saw a little bit of a raping when really it wasn't; I had her full consent," Blue said. putting his arms on Meganlynn. "Come, now, Annie."

"What did you just call me?"

"Oh, just come." They ran out of the police station and back out into the open road.

"Johnny!" she yelled as they pulled her away.

"Meganlynn!" he yelled back as he ran back the way that they were dragging Meganlynn. Meganlynn tried harder than ever to try and get loose from their grip, but she didn't have any luck. She screamed and scrambled all over the place and screamed every time they tried to tell her to shut her mouth. Johnny was running toward them, screaming for her and trying to grab her hand to pull her back every chance that he got. Justin finally grabbed her back around the waist and carried her back to the car where they threw her in. Blue jumped in the back seat with her, and Justin drove away.

"Johnny!" Meganlynn yelled one last time.

"Did you kiss him?"

"No," she answered. She knew that she had forgotten to do something that was really important.

"Good, the spell could still take effect."

"Yeah, right." Meganlynn pulled her mp3 player out of her purse and started to listen to it.

They drove for what seemed to be hours and hours, but it was really hours and hours. Meganlynn was placed in the back seat with her notebooks and everything else at her disposal. She did not know where she was going to go or anything like that, but she knew that she was wherever God had wanted her to be. She knew that she was there for a reason. She did not know whether her reason to be there was to beat the living crap out of him or what; she just knew that she was supposed to be there.

"When are we going to be there?" she asked them.

"Well, we are taking a plane out from the Chicago Airport, so you can tell me since we are in Chicago," Blue answered.

"I guess about five minutes, huh?"

"Yeah, pretty much." They pulled into the Chicago Airport. Meganlynn thought hard to herself. She knew that she needed to make her move now, or she would never get her chance to be free. She walked into the airport with Blue and Justin holding her hands.

Once they had finally arrived at the security checkpoint, Meganlynn saw the sign that said "Please remove all metal objects and take off your shoes." Meganlynn did just that. Other than taking out one of her earrings, she took out her pen from her purse and then wrote the words "help me" on her hands. She did not care if she was going to die or not; she only cared if she was going to get out of the clutches of Blue and Justin or not.

It was finally her turn to go through the machine. The alarm went off, and since Blue and Justin were both in front of her, she was taken aside and checked. The officer read both of her hands.

"Ma'am, please come with me…" he said, trailing off.

"Sir," she said as she was following him. "If there are two men following us, have them arrested they're the ones that kidnapped me."

"Okay," the security guard said as he turned around.

"Boys," he said, walking up to them as he gave Meganlynn to another security guard. "You need to come with me."

"Okay," Blue said, and they followed the officer until they were in a room separate from Meganlynn. The security guard pulled the door shut and locked behind them. Meganlynn sat down in the room, and then waited for the officer to come in.

The door opened and the officer walked in and sat down. He folded his hands and Meganlynn did the same.

"Now, the only way that you are not in trouble is if you are seriously in trouble."

"I am, sir."

"What is going on?"

"Have you heard about the missing person, Meganlynn VanDeritie?"

"Yes, I believe everyone has. Why are you asking me this?"

"Because I am Meganlynn VanDeritie."

"But—"

"We tried to tell the local police department last night but they kept on telling us that we had to have a appointment because the chief wasn't in at the moment. We told the lady out there that it was an emergency, and she didn't believe us. Then, she had the nerve to ask us if we knew where I was. I was about to tell her that I was Meganlynn VanDeritie, but Blue and Justin came back and took me back from where I was standing with Johnny."

"Well, then we can communicate with the local police department."

"May I call my parents?"

"Yes. Actually, can I call your parents, or Meganlynn's parents, to see if they can identify you as Meganlynn?"

"Yes, and if you want, you can call Johnny and ask him. They will all tell you that I am Meganlynn VanDeright."

"I will call the local police department because I have to."

"Okay." Meganlynn then sat back and then realized for the time that she had left.

Some time had passed, but not very much, before the local police were in the door. The police were in the doorway of the hallway. They took Blue and Justin after having taken Meganlynn's fingerprints. They really did not have enough proof, apparently, to have determined that she was actually Meganlynn VanDeritie. She really did not care; she just wanted to have her family and friends back in her life.

"Now, ma'am, you do understand that if your parents cannot recognize you, you will be charged with impersonating a missing person?"

"Yes, but I am her, I'm telling you the truth."

"I believe you, honey," the female police officer, Officer Gallery, said to her.

"Thank you, but how much longer until I can see my family?"

"When was the last time you saw them?"

"About five days ago."

"You miss them, don't you?"

"Very much."

"Then, where did Blue and Justin take you?"

"To a hotel in Detroit where we waited for prom night to come."

"What did they do to you on the day of prom?"

"They performed witchcraft on me." Meganlynn answered annoyed with the thought of it.

"Are you sure?"

"Yes, and they did not have my consent."

"Well, kidnapping, everything."

"They have done it all to me."

"You cannot be serious."

"I am serious. They have done, honestly, everything for the past three years to me."

"Well, we can get them on that."

"Thankfully."

"Yes, now did they threaten you?"

"Yes, Blue and Justin said that if I told anyone then he would kill my relatives, slowly. And then take pictures of them. He would then place me in a room with all of the pictures of my family members around me."

"Okay, that's not that weird, is it?" she asked sarcastically.

"Not at all."

"Wow."

"How long ago did my parents leave?"

"They should be here right about now." Meganlynn saw her parents walk through the doors of the airport. They ran up to the front desk and saw Johnny come in right behind them with their luggage. They were then sent into the room where Meganlynn was sitting.

"Mom!" she yelled once she was in the room. Her mother grasped on to her and would not let go.

"Meganlynn!" Her mother was crying because she had not seen her daughter, and she had been scared for her daughter's safety.

"Dad!" Meganlynn shouted, hugging her dad at the same time. He was also crying because he was so happy to see her again and alive.

"Meg," Johnny said as he walked over to her. He kissed her and let her go back to her parents who were still going through the time where they were extremely excited that they were going to have their daughter back and alive and well.

"I love you," her mother whispered in her right ear.

"I love you, too," Meganlynn answered back.

"I love you as well," her father then said into her left ear.

"I love you, too, Daddy," she told her father. Meganlynn was now crying also because she was so happy to be back in the arms of her family.

"Can I have her for one second?" Johnny asked her parents.

"Yes, that would be okay."

"Mr. and Mrs. VanDeritie, I need to speak to you," said Officer Gallery.

"Well, then I guess it really is okay."

"Meg, come here." Johnny took her over to the other side of the room.

"Johnny," she said, wrapping her arms around him and then kissing him again. He pulled out a little box that was bigger than a ring box but yet smaller than a bracelet box.

"What is this?" she asked him.

"Here, open it. Remember this day, time, hour, because this is one of the most important days of your life."

"Okay." She opened the box. Inside the box was a necklace, a ring, a bracelet, and two pairs of earrings. The necklace was gold with diamonds. The charm that came down off the necklace was a golden heart with little diamonds surrounding it. The dangly pair of earrings was made of real diamonds as well. There were small, sapphire hearts in the middle of the circle of diamonds that went around it. Then, the second pair of earrings were big, golden hoops that had a diamond in the middle of each of them. Then the ring was absolutely beautiful with two heart-shaped sapphires and two diamond chips on either side of them. The ring its self was white gold.

The bracelet was the most beautiful thing that anyone could have ever given her. It was a golden charm bracelet that had charms already on it. The hearts on the bracelet interlocked with one another to form the bracelet. Meganlynn then looked back up at him as if to say, "Wow, you got me all of this?"

"I got you the bracelet, and the charms each mean something special. I got you the airplane charm because this is where we found you. I got you the bear and the fawn because of how soft and nice you are to other people and your friends. I got you the dove, angel wings, angel with two hearts, and the Bible because of your religious views, and I knew that you would want those on there. I got you the swan, flowers, and butterfly because of your beauty. I got you the merry-go-round horse, the carriage, and the merry-go-round because of how fun you are to be around. I got you the book, the working desk, and the typewriter because of the writer that you are. I got you the boots, dancers, and the trombone because of your love for music and because you play the trombone. I got you the two hearts charm because of the love that we have for one another. Here." He then placed it on her wrist. "I will never let you out my sight again."

Meganlynn, Johnny, and her parents then went into the lobby area. After talking to some more of the officers that were taking care of the case, they were then allowed to leave and go home.

Meganlynn jumped on her old bed with her old pajamas and then laid there after they had gotten home.

Johnny walked into the room where she was laying. He knew that she didn't have to go to school for the next week.

"You want to watch a movie with your family?"

"Yeah, I would love to as long as you sit with me."

"No, I think I'm going to sit with your mom."

"Johnny," she said as she walked up to him and placed her arms around his waist. She kissed him again.

"Maybe I'm okay with you missing me this much."

"Very funny, Johnny, very funny."

"Let's go watch the movie before your parents get suspicious."

"Okay." They went to the living room and watched the movie with her parents as they all cuddled in front of the fireplace, watching the television.

CHAPTER 12

It had been two months since Meganlynn was rescued from the clutches of Blue and Justin. The trial may have been only about two days away, but this day was Meganlynn and Johnny's graduation day.

Everything was even more hectic at their house since Johnny and Meganlynn's graduation parties were on the same day and at the same time. Johnny's family was staying there with her family. His two sisters were sharing a room with Meganlynn. Johnny was stretched out on the couch, and his parents were in his room. He was quiet when getting his clothes because he did not want to wake them up. They had the run of the house while Meganlynn's parents were not at home. They had the run of the neighborhood as well.

It was finally time for Johnny and Meganlynn's graduation to begin. Meganlynn was asked to make a speech about what had happened to her over the past three years.

They arrived at the school and went inside to get ready for graduation. Everyone got into the lines that they would be in to march down the aisle as they were going to get their diplomas. Finally, the music started.

"Meganlynn," Johnny whispered from the back.

"Yes?" she asked.

"Do you have your bracelet on?"

"I have the bracelet, necklace, and earrings on right now."

"You do?"

"I need my good luck charms."

"Are they good luck charms because I gave them to you?"

"Yeah." Her name came over the loud speaker. "That's me," she said as she walked through the curtains to the stage.

Finally, once everyone had been announced, everyone sat down and all of the teachers made their speeches. It was time for the valedictorian to make her speech. The valedictorian was one of Meganlynn's closet friends: Taylor VanFork.

"Not all of you know me, but I am Taylor VanFork. I am, somehow, the valedictorian for the class of two thousand ten. How I got to be here, I have no clue. I know that I really want to be a vet and I know that my good friends all want to be something that has a link to college experiences. I know that Lizzie wants to be a physiologist, Morgan wants to be a fashion designer, and Johnny wants to be a lawyer, and Meganlynn wants to be an investigative journalist because she can write like no one even knows. No one in this class has been through as much in this year as one girl has in their entire life. She has a special speech that she wants to make that will explain more about that.

All I know is that these past four years here have been amazing years for me, and I hope that everyone was able to feel that very same way about this school. People were changed here, people were made to be friendly that were never friendly in the first place. They were given friends that no one ever thought that they would get. They were given encouragement that no one ever thought that they would have because they were weird or mean or something like that. Most people like that had girlfriends that actually looked at the inside and not at the outside. This class is an amazing class and everyone should love them no matter what. Congrats class of two thousand ten!"

"Well, that was an amazing speech Ms. VanFork. Now, from this speech, there may be tears from a lot of the audience and from the speaker herself. She has many stories that she can tell from the many experiences that she has had from these past four years. Never has this girl complained, and all of her grades were awesome. She was never the type to complain that she had this type of situation. This is an amazing girl, and she was never going to tell anyone because they had threatened her. If anyone ever has these same experiences that this young lady has ever had, I feel really bad for you because you are going through a lot. If you are going through the same things, you should go and tell someone no matter what you are being threatened. Now, for the speech that you all have been waiting for: Ms. Meganlynn VanDeritie." The audience clapped. Video cameras came up, and cameras went up as well. Meganlynn tried to imagine that she was just back in her room trying to practice this speech over this.

"Hello," she said. "Okay, I got my first word out." The crowd giggled. "Now, I am up here to tell you about my experiences about the past four years of this high school. Many people go through high school as being the cheerleader, the jock, emo, or preppy, but me, on the other hand, I was the one that should have been the person that was the true emotional Goth, or anything that was dark. I wasn't a cutter or anything like that. I couldn't feel anything good except my boyfriend, friends, and family. Other than that, my experience here was horrible.

"The only thing that was good was that my boyfriend, friends, and family, were always there for me. I used to be raped often here at school, and no matter what, they were ones that were there protecting me. Johnny used to stand in front of them until they would finally leave me alone. If it wasn't Blue, it was Justin. They may have started off as one of the popular people, and two of the hottest guys in school, but nothing ever gave them the right to take everything away from me.

"Blue did anything and everything to me. Blue raped, beat, stalked, sexually harassed, and did just about everything else to me. I was scared to death that he was going to kill me, so much so that I even forgot that my book got published for about a month and a half. I urge anyone and everyone that is going through any of the things that I just mentioned to tell someone because of the emotional toil that has put me through. I hope that the right person is prosecuted.

"Now, the only thing that I have left to say is this: I faced the pain, I faced the trial, all these things that have happened to me have happened for a reason. I just wish that I knew the reason why it all happened. Yet, I think that I do know the reason that this all happened was because I am not going to face trials harder than this or similar to this. I think that this trial was to show me how strong I truly was. I know that people who are atheists cannot know what real love is because they know not what real love is. The real love is called God. I'm sorry if I have offended you in some way, but all who are old enough to make the decision between right and wrong are old enough to hear the true gospel of Jesus Christ our Lord and Savior.

"The class of two thousand and ten sure is a great one, and I hope that you all make good decisions. Let your next experiences be the greatest for you. Thank you." The crowd roared for Meganlynn as she walked off of the stage.

Once all of the graduates were off the stage, Meganlynn and Johnny met up with their families outside the school.

"You did great, sweetie," Meganlynn's mother told her, squeezing her.

"Thanks, Mom, did you get it on videotape?"

"You bet."

They hugged.

After everyone had started leaving, Meganlynn and Johnny were on their way out the door when Taylor, Lizzie, and Morgan came by with a car. Meganlynn and

Johnny looked at their parents as if to ask them if they could go with them.

"Go ahead and go," Meganlynn's parents told her.

"You too, Johnny," his parents told him. Meganlynn and Johnny grabbed what they needed out of the car and hopped into the car with their friends and went off to celebrate their graduation before Meganlynn had to go to Blue's trial.

CPSIA information can be obtained at www.ICGtesting.com
Printed in the USA
LVOW08s2227290813

350295LV00002B/76/P